DAMSEL

&

ROGERS

To Janet
with love & thanks

Trinity
Damsel
x

ISBN-13: 978-1499722468

ISBN-10:149972246X

Cover Art by Violet Fox. Thanks, Violet! *swak*

www.damselandrogers.com
www.facebook.com/damselandrogers

DEDICATION

This book is dedicated to all the men & women who have touched upon our lives and contributed to our sexual experiences, especially one special person that visited Paris with Trinity – you know who you are.

CHAPTER ONE

As Zara lay in the bath, she watched the bubbles that covered her breasts pop as her warm breath played delicious games with her nipples. Her mind drifted back to this time last year in Jamaica, where she had lounged on the beach with the sun gently massaging the warm breeze against her golden skin. Oh, for more moments like those, she needed them now; these memories were all she had of her much needed holiday last year.

She pulled her languid body up to sit in the bath and viewed herself. Her skin had lost the Jamaican sun long ago but the firm, smooth texture still remained. She remembered the short time spent with one of the Jamaicans playing volleyball on the beach. The fun she had had, discovering the secrets of his body; how he reacted to her hot, slow tongue, finding even the smallest hole to delve into. She had not had the pleasure of another body since then and was feeling a little frustrated. Work had taken over this year, leaving her little time for socialising which had resulted in her being too busy to even contemplate sharing her precious time with a 'mate'.

Zara sank under the bubbles, her long dark hair floating over her shoulders as she reached for the soap. The lather from the soap made the bubbles disappear as she slowly massaged her breasts.

The massage started from the outside and worked in towards her, now erect, nipples. The slow provocative movements increased her pleasure. Her nipples, now in full bud, pleaded to be touched but she teased herself, enjoying being the one in control of her own body. She imagined the Jamaican's mouth hovering above the hard bud, teasing her, wanting her, begging him to suck and nibble her nipples. Now she was in control, she didn't have to beg herself; she could bring herself to climax whenever she wanted – but oh! How she missed the feel of somebody else's skin against her own.

One hand left the breast it had been fondling and slid down her rib cage and onto her thighs, between her thighs. She brought her knees up above the water and parted them so that they touched the cold enamel of the bath; her fingers strolled along her pubic hair, entwining the dark curls that hid her most precious pleasure. As she parted the silken doorway her index finger caught the tip of her clitoris, it swelled with anticipation, sending a shiver through her body and her back arched in response... Preep, Preep! Preep, Preep! The mobile phone shattered the moment immediately. Zara shot up in surprise and cursed "Bollocks!" she said clicking on the phone. "Hello Zara Hardcastle speaking. How may I help you?" The telephone manner switched on with professional ease.

"You can cut that crap out, it's me," the familiar voice replied.

"Jo, you could have called later, this is a most inopportune moment."

"Why? Are you on the bog?"

"No! I was, uhm, in the middle of something; it doesn't matter now, I can go back to it later. What's up?" Zara asked as she stepped out of the bath and wrapped a towel around herself, thinking that she must definitely return to her pleasures later.

"It's not important really; I just thought I'd give you a ring to ask you if you knew anyone who would like seven days in Paris, free?"

"Oh yeah, what's the catch?" Zara asked suspiciously.

"There's none, unless you count me as a travel partner a catch."

Jo was Zara's oldest friend from school days and she loved her to pieces but she could be rather coarse at times. When they were younger they used to double-date and go clubbing together, this was before Zara had chosen her career path; over the last few years Zara had had little time for social pleasures, unless they were connected to her employment. Jo did make Zara laugh and Zara missed this.

"Where did you get a trip to Paris from?" Zara asked, doubting that it was really free.

"I saved up the tokens on my cat food tins, smart eh?"

Zara caught the smug tone in Jo's voice and thought, that's why she liked her so much, "Nobody but you would manage to get a holiday from a cat. Who are you taking with you?"

"You, you silly bugger. That's if it's not beneath you to take a holiday from a cat. I know it's only Paris and you're used to a more foreign climate…"

This triggered Zara's thoughts once again of Jamaica and her overseas love affair bringing a blush of guilty pleasure to her cheeks.

"Oh Jo, I'd love to come. When is it?"

"A week on Friday; the coach picks us up from Leicester and takes us overnight on the ferry, then the coach arrives in Paris Saturday. We head for home on the following Friday, arriving back in Leicester, Saturday afternoon. So get your clothes washed and sorted as we're off to Gay Paree in 2 weeks."

"I'm due some holiday time, so I'll clear it with my boss first and so long as it is okay by her, I'll give you a ring tomorrow night to confirm. Thanks for thinking of me Jo, I need this holiday, especially with you as you have such a wonderful way of lifting me up. I do so miss your company, you know."

"You need to loosen up and forget work for a while. They'll be plenty of fancy Frenchies over there, so many; you won't know which to choose."

"Are you suggesting I need a man to help me unwind?" Zara asked.

"You're turning the other way now are you? Well that's what friends are for." Jo said with a suggestive tone in her voice.

Zara grinned to herself and wondered if Jo would ever make good on her flirts.

"Speak to you tomorrow night then, bye." Jo hung up swiftly.

Too swiftly, Zara thought, leaving a small electrical charge in the air behind her. Zara had completely understood the suggestion in Jo's voice though, which led her now to turn her thoughts to Jo on a beach playing volley ball. Zara returned to the bath to finish what she had started with a different character playing the lead role this time.

Summer Lovin', had me a blast, summer lovin' happened so fast, Zara was woken rudely by John Travolta and Olivia Newton-John blasting out 'Summer Nights' at 6.30am. Who picks these records at this time in the morning she thought, bashing the switch to off and knocking her 'needs for Paris' list onto the floor. She had sat up in bed on the previous night jotting down some of the essentials that she must find time to get in her lunch break (if she was lucky enough to have time for a lunch break, that is). The week was even more hectic than normal as she was trying to leave everything in order so that the office ran smoothly whilst she was away. Her boss had been understanding and agreed that she needed a holiday. It had been nine months since she last had time off work due to the current demand for temps with varied secretarial skills. The strain was starting to show after ten hour six day weeks.

Zara arrived at work at 8.30am sharp, checked the memo tray for any messages and sat behind her desk to read them. Nothing important, work wise, but there was a note from her boss who was at a conference, instructing her to finish work early today (Thursday) and have tomorrow off. Zara had planned to work the Friday as the coach was not going to pick them up until late evening, so this was fantastic news; she would have time to do some more shopping and pack at a leisurely pace. She carried on reading the note as there was a short p.s. at the bottom:

> **Please, please, please find a man to relieve you, I hate all this pent up sexuality you're carrying with you - you need a good fuck! Have fun, love Sheila.**

Zara loved her work; her relationship with her boss was so informal. Sheila was married with three children and was a very wise woman. She could 'feel' when things were not right and she could always sense Zara's moods.

Zara let her mind wander. Do I really need a man; is it so obvious that I'm showing pent up sexuality? Just the thought of sex aroused her. This was terrible, I'm at work, she thought and it was only a quarter to nine. Am I so sex-starved that I have fantasies at my desk? Just then her eyes spotted the smooth, cold, phallus shaped paper-weight on her desk. She picked it up and felt the coolness run through her fingers. Her body ached for penetration. Yes she was indeed that sex-starved, it seemed.

In a decisive, cool manner she got up and walked to the door. She looked through the glass panels and she saw her admin busy typing so she pulled the cord to close the dusky pink blinds and quietly turned the key to lock the door. What she planned to do, she planned to do alone. She turned around and calmly returned to her desk. Spinning her swivel chair to face away from the window, Zara sat leaning back in the chair so that her lower body was tipped forward towards the edge of the seat. Parting her legs, she slowly ran her fingers up her thighs, hiking her skirt up to her hips and slipping the flimsy lace pants to one side of her moist maiden hair. Her fingers parted the warm lips and with her other hand she clasped the paper-weight and inserted its tip into the moisture. Oh Christ! This is what her body had been crying out for, for weeks, and she had not listened to it.

The coolness just excited her more and she pushed it slowly deeper until she felt her muscles contract on it, she was trying to suck it deeper into her very depths; she wanted all of it, no teasing, just hard and fast. Now. Her wrist started to pump the instrument. As she moved faster and faster, each thrust made her hips respond in time to meet the hard, cool pleasure of her chosen stimulus. She could feel the sensations of an orgasm starting; the warm gush flowed through her veins and her toes went rigid, followed by her legs and hips, then her heart started to beat double time. Here it is, she thought, release. She cried out as her breathing became uncontrollable, her body convulsed and in spasms the orgasm overtook her body.

She slumped against her chair and became conscious of her surroundings again. Her breathing started to slow and she slowly removed the phallus, which sent a small tingle through her nerve endings on its departure. She realised that Sheila's words were true, she *was* full of sexual tension and she knew now that she was a woman who needed a man. After all, men were easier to find than phallus shaped paper-weights.

Zara straightened her clothing, went to the ladies, concealing her 'mate' in her handbag and washed away any evidence of her five minute pleasure. She returned to her office and placed the paper-weight over the memo from her boss, writing below the message:

> **Don't worry Sheila, I'll be back in a week, released from tension. Look after the office and make sure no one touches the items on my desk - they're very precious to me.**
>
> **Love Zara.**

The rest of the day flew past and Zara knocked off work at the normal time. When she left her office she said goodbye to 'Mark' standing proudly erect on her desk as the first to enter her in a very long time. She was ready for her getaway and was definitely looking forward to what her future in Paris might hold for her.

CHAPTER TWO

The coach was not too bad; they had a fair amount of leg room and there was a toilet, which Jo refused to use as she told Zara that she was sure it would leave a trail behind her on the road, but was there nonetheless. The other passengers were of mixed types: the usual tourists comprised of two families, both with spotty teenagers who were always complaining; an old couple who played travel backgammon throughout the journey; and several young couples who were either sleeping or fondling each other.

"No single males here, they must all be waiting for us on the ferry," Jo said hopefully.

Zara and Jo passed the time by inventing names for the other passengers and flicking through magazines to find the problem pages. Jo liked to be 'Aunty Jo' and give answers to all the anxieties printed. As usual she managed to make Zara laugh and Zara felt herself slowly unwinding.

After three stops, for relief and sustenance, the coach arrived at Dover. The driver, who Jo had named 'Dick, nice but thick', told the passengers on what deck level they were parked and at what time they must board the coach the following morning. He wished them all a pleasant crossing and went to find the bar.

"He's done this before," Zara commented "Shall we freshen up and do the same?"

They went into the ferry and passed several eating places and a couple of bars.

"Look over there, an all night disco. Are you game?" Jo asked with great enthusiasm.

The word 'disco' brought images of Zara's school days into her head, with flashes of dark corners and first thrills, along with spotty pubescent boys and fizzy bottled drinks. "We didn't sleep much on the coach. I could do with a lie down first. Where's our cabin?" "Cabin? You don't get that with 'cat food holidays', you sleep where you fall," Jo said dragging Zara into the ladies toilets and heading for the first cubicle. "I'm going to change into something more comfortable," Jo shouted from behind the door.

While Jo was busy getting comfortable, Zara rummaged through her bag for some fresh wipes and found them wedged between her make-up bag and a large packet of condoms, one of the 'essentials' for the trip. She felt very clammy from the long coach trip and would have preferred a shower and a change of underwear, but needs must when the devil drives.

Jo came out of the cubicle and viewed herself in the mirror, smoothing down her skin-tight dress and inspecting her figure.

Zara watched her stroke her hands slowly over the lycra material, covering all the curves on her body and found herself fascinated by her breasts. Zara could see Jo's nipples hardening and pushing their way forward through the material. Zara shared Jo's excitement; it felt like they were both back in the girls' room of their school disco.

"Look good, do I?" Jo asked Zara's reflection in the mirror.

Zara had not realised that Jo could see her watching and embarrassed, but aroused, replied, "You look fantastic Jo and I for one appreciate your curves." Zara gave a cheeky wink as she turned to go into a cubicle herself.

'Get a grip Zara,' she told herself, 'you need a man and you're going to find one tonight. If Jo can be so confident, so can you.' With this thought she slipped her pants down, took them off and threw them in the bin. Now she felt refreshed and ready for anything.

"Come on then Zara. I'm ready, are you?" Jo shouted through the door. 'This is the start of fun and flirtations and it's all thanks to my moggy eating so much. Let's show 'em what we're made of."

Zara opened the door and walked out towards Jo. "I'm ready for anything," she said in a husky voice and with a naughty wink.

It had been nearly a year since Zara had had any flirtatious fun and she felt a little nervous of the prospect of male interest in her. She had invitations and passes made her way but she had either ignored or declined them all, as she was too busy working her way up the career ladder. Soon she was going to be playing the mating game again and she was not sure whether she had the confidence to really do it anymore. Outwardly she looked confident but inwardly she felt the butterflies' wings flicking around her insides; luckily this fear was exciting her even more.

Jo squeezed Zara's hand reassuringly and caught her eyes with her own, "Zara don't worry. I'm here. We're going to have fun. You look fantastic and really sexy. Come on."

Zara smiled, "Thanks Jo," she said and taking a deep breath, checked herself in the mirror. "Right. I'm ready."

They left the ladies and entered the bar. Jo's eyes trawled the room for a possible catch, "There's Fred but dead, slumped over the bar," Jo said indicating an old man that looked the worse for wear. Jo took the lead and pulled Zara towards the bar. "Two 'J.D's' and coke please." Jo asked the barmaid as she handed the money over, "Is there any talent here tonight?"

"Talent! You must be joking. The ugly ones are in here getting plastered and the good-lookers are outside throwing up. Get a few more of them inside you," the barmaid said passing the drinks to Jo. "And they'll all look irresistible. Try the disco for 'talent'."

They walked across the bar towards the entrance to the disco. It was packed and Zara could feel the atmosphere of the place just standing by the door. Hot bodies were pressed close, soft lights enhanced moist lips, fast music produced fast movements, and the assortment of scents gathered and amassed at Zara's nostrils, leaving her feeling light-headed.

Jo moved inside and slinked her way between the moving bodies until she found a small space, where she could see and be seen. Zara watched her friend and admired her confidence; she used to be like that herself, before her career had taken over. She was now realising that there was more to life than earning money and making a name for herself in her occupation. She needed this to discover the Zara that had been hiding modestly away and was glad that it was Jo that was going to help her reveal the inner Zara, the one who would have a life out of work.

Zara followed the path that Jo had taken and joined her. Jo was moving to the music and ready to dance but Zara stood and sipped her drink, watching the other dancers. She would dance later, she told herself, especially if they played reggae. She loved the beat of reggae music and especially the drums; it affected her internally with her very inner senses responding to the low rhythmic beats and when she danced she felt native and sensual.

A small dark man asked Jo to dance and she moved away amongst the bodies with him, leaving Zara alone to soak up the ambience. Zara watched the dancers crammed together on the small dance floor, so close to each other no one could tell who was partnered with whom. Zara watched Jo enjoying herself, laughing at something the man had whispered to her.

"Hi I'm Noel. You look a bit lonely among all these bodies, so I thought you might like some company."

Zara turned towards the voice and faced a tall, slim young man with the most amazing eyes that seemed to envelope and protect her with just a single glance. Zara's face must have betrayed her appreciation of his attention as he placed his hand on her arm and asked her if she would like to dance. This was heaven sent; she now had a chance to be confident and regain her sexuality with a man that was definitely of her liking. She walked with him onto the dance floor.

The space available to each dancer was about a square foot and therefore there were plenty of chances to make physical contact with someone, whether wanted or not; yet Noel kept his distance. They danced together without talking for three records, then the music style changed and an old punk record started playing.

"I don't like this stuff, let's go and sit somewhere," Noel said touching Zara's arm to lead her off the dance floor.

Zara was enjoying herself now and didn't want to leave, so she pretended that she had not heard him and moved her arms up above her head, carrying on dancing. Jo appeared by her side and copied Zara's dance movements and they danced in unison like a pair of teenagers, throwing their arms around wildly and bouncing up and down with their heads ducking and darting.

When the record finished, Jo told Zara that she had met a very 'suitable' young man and was going to be spending some time with him, if Zara didn't mind. Zara felt quite happy to be alone and told Jo to go and enjoy herself as she was going to get another drink and then dance some more. They agreed to meet up before the ferry docked, and then parted.

Zara finished her drink and returned to the dance floor. The music kept changing and Zara kept dancing, quite unaware that there were several dancers eyeing up her body's movements. The reggae duly arrived and Zara became lost in a world of her own.

'*Tease me tease me till I lose control,*' the singer begged and Zara's body moved with the beat; her hips and pelvis gyrating invitingly. The dance floor filled up and there was barely enough room to move but Zara didn't notice as she was in a world of her own.

Pulled out of her trance-like state, Zara felt a body behind her, pushed tightly up against her, moving with her. It was definitely male as she could feel his erection pushing against her lower back. He was keeping in perfect time with her movements, so that they were moving as one.

And it felt so good. His hands slid onto Zara's hips as she rolled them around and then they moved onto her backside and stroked her buttocks with the flow of the music. She wanted to turn around and see the face of this exquisite mover but was afraid she might be disappointed, so she carried on dancing and let the music and her imagination take her where it would.

She felt the anonymous hand raise the back of her skirt and slide his fingers between her thighs. She was so turned on by the music and this new thrill that she did not prevent him; nobody could see, she knew, as his body was thrust against hers, hiding any bare flesh that could have been exposed. His fingers discovered that she was wearing no knickers and she caught an intake of breath in her ear from her strange mover, and his body rubbed her back more forcefully, giving her an intimate outline of his erection.

The beat of the record continued relentlessly and the stranger inserted his thumb and moved it with the rhythm. Zara could feel herself responding to this and not to the beat of the music; she was dancing on his thumb and urging it deeper and faster. The stranger responded to Zara's need by placing a finger on her clitoris and started moving the two in unison, flicking one whilst plunging the other.

Zara felt her insides start to warm and knew that she was on the brink of an orgasm but was so involved with the rhythms that she let it happen. The man knew that she was on the edge of her climax and held her tightly with his other arm as though guiding her through her pleasures and protecting her on her way. When she reached her peak, the music pounded out faster, as though applauding Zara for her actions.

The stranger pulled down her skirt, kissed her neck and whispered for her not to turn around; Zara felt his arms leave her and became conscious of the other bodies around her; nobody was interested; nobody had seen anything unusual. Had she imagined it?

The music changed to a slow romantic song and Zara glanced around the room for her stranger, but as she had no idea of what he looked like and only what he felt like, she was at a loss. Nobody was eyeing her as though they knew her, so she presumed her man had left or it had really all been a dream and she had got so involved with the music that she had imagined the whole thing.

Zara smoothed her skirt down and checked her dress was undisturbed then walked around the dancers to the way out, and to breathe some fresh air. The moon was up and it was quite chilly with the sea breeze blowing through her thin blouse. She strolled along the deck, past the lovers looking into each other's eyes, past the sickies with their heads over the side making retching noises and on towards the prow of the boat.

The night was beautiful, or was it just that she was glowing from her dance encounter? She leant over the side and looked at the moonlight glistening on the black water and was cast back yet again to a time in Jamaica when she had walked along the water's edge, barefoot in the sand with her volleyball man, where they made love amongst the ripples of the incoming tide.

"Hello again, are you enjoying the view? You look cold. Here take my jacket." It was Noel her punk hating friend from the disco.

"Thank you," Zara said as she wrapped his jacket over her shoulders, catching the smell of Aramis aftershave as she did. "I was just thinking about Jamaican nights and comparing them with this one," Zara felt a little guilty about the way that she had treated him on the dance floor earlier and tried to make polite conversation with him to make amends.

"Jamaica, that's where Reggae and Ska originate from isn't it?"

Zara looked at him and felt her cheeks redden. Was this her dance stranger, Noel, the one that was cool and polite? I don't think so she thought. His gaze gave her nothing to go on; he didn't look like he was keeping a secret but equally he didn't 'look' like the sort of man that would move so sensually. She dismissed the thought out of hand.

"Are you on holiday too?" Zara asked him, to change the conversation.

"No. I'm on business. I have to look at Paris fashions and check out any of the new fabrics that the designers may be using. My company designs and manufactures lingerie, and we have to keep an eye on the market for new designs and fabrics."

"Oh, that sounds like an exciting job; I bet you get to see all of the new designs before they are released for sale."

"Yes, we do normally but I'll be a bit late for the shows this month as I was due to fly over to Paris early this morning, but someone forgot to book my flight and I'm stuck with ferry and car transport. Not so luxurious is it?"

Zara then told Noel of Jo's perseverance with cat food labels and their free trip to Paris and how she was looking forward to seeing the sights. They started to walk along the deck whilst Noel told Zara more about his work. Zara was enjoying his company and felt glad that destiny had had a hand in him catching the ferry the same time as she had. Her initial thoughts about him were evolving; she wasn't sure whether it was because she thought he had been her secret lover, or simply because he was so sweet and gentlemanly. They strolled along and stopped by the railing to look out over the dark sea. The twinkle of the boat's lights reflected in the water.

"This is a nice break from work," sighed Noel gazing out to sea. Zara looked at him whilst he spoke and again felt herself attracted to him. She tried to imagine him naked; he was wearing a suit, with an Armani label and his shirt was made of finely woven fabric that covered every contour of his chest without clinging, teasing Zara's mind as to what he looked like unclothed. She imagined his skin to be a golden brown, naturally golden not from the sun and she could see he had broad shoulders and a flat stomach by the cut of his clothes.

"How long are you expecting to stay in Paris?" she asked hoping she might see him there.

"As long as it takes really, I never know what I might find." He walked towards a covered seating area and sat down, inviting Zara to sit beside him.

Zara sat. She would not mind meeting this man again, she thought. He was such a gentleman and she bet he knew all the right places to take a girl to in Paris. Not once had he made a sexual advance towards her and this did make a change from the men she had known in the past. But not so deep down she wished he would; she would not object to a steamy bit of passion in a cabin on the boat, or even in a hotel room in France. Even if she wasn't able to shag him before they landed at France, she sincerely hoped this would not be her only opportunity to share some moments of intimacy with him.

"Where has your friend got to? Are you supposed to be meeting her?" Noel asked, breaking Zara's reverie.

"She was with someone, the last time I saw her. In fact I ought to go and wait for her inside." Zara got up and handed Noel his jacket back. "Thank you for the loan, it should be warmer inside."

Noel stood also and suggested they find somewhere peaceful to wait and offered to keep her company to deter any unwelcome drunks.

Zara let him lead the way; she thought that he was an old fashioned gentleman and he made her feel very special. She had only had one steady boyfriend, when she was at school, and he had been possessive and immature; and her other short relationships had been few and far between. No one had put her needs before their own, or make her feel as feminine and special as Noel was making her feel now. This was a first for her and she was relishing the extra attention being shown towards her.

They found a seat for two, large enough for Zara to put her feet up.

"I'm feeling a bit tired, I hope you don't mind if I start to doze off," she told Noel. "Only we didn't get much sleep on the coach."

"Make yourself comfortable," Noel said, offering himself as a cushion.

Zara laid her head on his shoulder as they chatted about the places that she could visit whilst in Paris, finding a mutual interest in Notre Dame and its legends.

As the night went on and France got ever nearer, Zara dozed off nestling on Noel's chest and breathing in his male scent. This man's presence and coolness turned her on; it felt familiar as though she had known him in a previous existence and it felt comforting to be with him.

CHAPTER THREE

"The ferry will dock at Calais in approximately fifteen minutes. Could passengers please make their ways to their vehicles," the announcer boomed over the tannoy, waking Zara from her sleep.

The arm that was wrapped around her reminded her of the stranger on the dance floor and for a moment she felt confused. 'This arm feels so familiar, so reassuring, do I ask him if he was the stranger? If I do and it was not him, what will he think of me? Engaging in sexual play on a dance floor with a stranger is not the norm for me.'

Thoughts raced through Zara's mind as she wondered about this man, she ended with one magical thought and a secret smile crossed her lips, 'If it were him, his were the expert fingers that had given her so much pleasure.' She sat up and faced Noel, he was smiling at her and she thought those deep blue eyes could penetrate her thoughts.

"I hope you were not too uncomfortable with me laying on you," Zara said running her fingers through her long black hair, trying to make herself look a little more appealing after a few hours sleep in a public lounge.

"Don't tidy yourself up. You look beautifully sleepy," Noel said taking her hand away from her hair. "Just the sort of woman I would love to wake up with on a..." the rest of the sentence was cut short as Jo suddenly bounced up with a big grin on her face and asked Zara to hurry up as they would miss the coach.

Zara looked at Jo with a frown and said, "You go and grab our seats and I'll follow in a minute." Jo took her cue, winked cheekily and promptly disappeared as fast as she had bounced up.

"Well, we'd both better get to our vehicles then," Noel said as he stood up and took Zara's hand, helping her to her feet. "Thank you for a lovely time spent on a tedious crossing. I hope you have a wonderful holiday," he said with such politeness that seemed to change the earlier moment of closeness, abruptly, to a stranger's distance.

This cool manner put Zara on guard and she responded with equal politeness, "Thank you. I have enjoyed your company too. I hope your business in Paris is fruitful."

With the niceties now said, there was an embarrassing silence between them. Zara looked at her watch so that she could avoid those penetrating blue eyes, lest they see what she was really feeling. "Goodbye then," Noel said and leant forward to give her a simple kiss on her cheek.

As he did Zara turned her head and the kiss landed on her neck. The feel of his warm, firm lips brought back a host of earlier feelings; they reminded her of the lips that had nuzzled her neck in the disco and a hot, electrical bolt of sexual energy shot through Zara's body when the realisation became clear. She looked up into his eyes and received a blue, knowing twinkle from them in return. Zara's body was on fire, she felt embarrassed and aroused at the same time.

"Goodbye," Zara said and turned quickly to avoid any further embarrassment and headed for the lower decks and her coach.

The coach trip from Calais to Paris passed enjoyably as Jo related her exploits. She had met a French man, who was returning from a holiday in Wales - apparently that was all she had managed to find out about him as they had been too busy having oral sex in one of the lifeboats to bother about social niceties.

"We couldn't move about much as the dinghy kept swaying, so he went down on me and I later returned the compliment. These Frenchmen really know how to give head Zara, you'll have to find one, it was fantastic - and he knew where my secret button was without me having to guide him."

Zara smiled and thought that Noel was English and by the way his fingers moved the last thing he needed was guidance.

"What's that secret smile for. What have you been up to?" Jo asked but was given only a laugh in reply.

The coach dropped everyone off outside of the hotel and 'Dick nice but thick' told them that he would be back that evening to give them a tour of the 'red light' district, nod, nod, wink, wink, and the holiday-makers could view it from the safety of their coach. Zara and Jo looked at each other and both read the other's mind which said, *'We'll skip that one then shall we'.*

They went into the hotel and collected their key to room 324. There was no lift in the hotel so they lugged their crammed suitcases up the three floors and arrived outside their room exhausted, hot and ready for a shower and a lie down.

Zara opened the door and they walked in. Inside was a clean, simply furnished room with an en-suite shower room. The furnishings were very floral and consisted of a settee, a table, two chairs, a double wardrobe and a double bed. They both looked at the bed and burst out laughing.

"It'll have to be split shifts for the bed if we need to entertain," Jo said. "Mind you, It'll mean sleeping together, which I don't mind in the slightest," Zara caught a darkening in Jo's eyes as her pupils enlarged sensually which stopped as she changed the mood with, "You don't snore do you?"

Zara laughed huskily as she was also imagining a bedtime with Jo and the feel of her curvaceous body alongside her own, "No I don't and I hope you don't either or else it's the settee for you," Zara looked at Jo straight in the eyes and said, "I wonder what other surprises this cat food holiday will bring." Zara completed this with a sexy wink.

They took it in turn to shower. Whilst Jo showered, Zara unpacked her clothes. She unfolded an all-in-one black lace garment that she had brought with her and thought; I wonder if the company that Noel works for designed this. She loved sexy underwear; it always made her feel sensual when she was wearing something 'naughty' under her ordinary clothes.

When all her clothes were put away in the wardrobe and drawers, she undressed for her shower.

Jo returned from her shower, rubbing her hair with a towel, "That was fantastic, the water's like needles. It really refreshes you. What I need most is a long sleep. I didn't get any last night." Jo noticed Zara standing naked in front of her and stood looking at her intimately, "Wow! Zara, you have the most amazing body, you ought to show it off a bit more. Wear some figure hugging clothes and draw some attention to those curves."

Zara picked up a towel and wrapped it around her, feeling a little modest by Jo's compliment. For so long she had been too busy with her work to care about how her clothes looked, other than smart and business-like. 'I don't really have anything like that,' she said somewhat self-consciously.

"'I've got a lace dress that would really suit you. We are going to have to change your image back to match the old Zara, which I know still exists and that this holiday will hopefully help you to find," Jo said as she opened the wardrobe to look at Zara's clothes hanging neat and organised. "Did you bring *anything* sexy with you?" Jo asked.

Zara gave herself a mental shake as she took her eyes off the clothes and listened to what Jo was saying, "Not really Jo. My problem is that I have been so busy smashing the glass ceiling at work that I've got pretty used to only wearing suits, not really all that sexy. And anyway, I'll need some more confidence to remove that image before I start up another."

Jo walked to the bed and flopped backwards onto it, she looked shattered. "After I've had a sleep and recharged my batteries, I am going to make you look so gorgeous that you will feel like a sex goddess." And with that, Jo snuggled her way under the blankets and drifted into sleep.

Zara left Jo and went into the shower thinking about what her friend had said. She really did need to feel good about herself again. She wanted to enjoy her body and be self assured; after all she was now in control of her work life and was well respected there. As for her social life, that was practically nonexistent; she just needed some fun again and judging by the ferry incident, fun was what this holiday was all about. Zara smiled at her naked reflection in the bathroom mirror and told it, 'Lighten up girl!' Then she stepped into the shower and let the needles of water cleanse her of all the work related thoughts.

After the shower, she walked back into the bedroom and saw Jo already fast asleep with her hair spread on the pillow in damp curls around her face. 'She looks like a small child,' Zara thought, 'but maybe not so innocent.'

She took off her towel and climbed into bed looking at the clock on the wall. It was 4.30pm; she closed her eyes and was gone into a world of dreams.

The tongue trailed its way up Zara's inner thigh, whilst the hands gently raised her knees and parted her legs. She felt the smooth skin of a body between her legs and the hot breath getting nearer to the place that was luring the tongue, into its dark, deep secret. It reached the black silken hair that covered the doorway to its goal and with a few flicks from side to side managed to gain access by parting the outer protective folds. Zara shivered and felt her nipples respond to the stimulus; she reached up to satisfy her nipples' need and started to encircle them with her thumbs. The tongue pushed its way up between the outer folds and found the hard nub of the deep pink guard, standing erect protecting the inner doorway. The tongue teased and taunted the guard with slow circular movements, trailing around the swollen folds of flesh; it was trying to bribe its way in. Zara let out a deep moan and parted her legs wider, offering herself to the tongue. This was just the excuse that the tongue needed and the mouth made its attack; it surrounded the guard and lowered its warmth over the hard nub, sucking the pinkness. Zara felt like she was going to explode; this felt so good, it was as if a sex fairy had cast a delicious spell on her and she was in dream heaven. The mouth continued to work its magic, using the edges of its teeth to give more forceful stimulation. A thumb joined in, rubbing the outside of the inner doorway, slowly working along the dark tunnel of paradise, bringing Zara ever closer to her orgasm. The tongue and its accomplice were now in control; the guard's defences were down and it was open and eager for attack. Zara's breathing increased, her moans became louder, she started to rub her breasts and roughly pull at her erect nipples; she was so close and she needed this so badly. The mouth sucked and licked at the moist lips, whilst the tongue shot in and out of the tunnel with sharp, hard movements. Zara felt the walls of her tunnel contract as the spasms overtook her body. She was sent on sexual wave after sexual wave and heard herself cry out as the orgasm overtook her mind and her body, leaving her subject to the compulsive muscular movements that she could not control. The tongue and mouth pulled away from the guard and the tunnel, as they knew it had crossed the point of no return.

Zara opened her eyes, it was dusky evening and she could make out her knees in the darkness and the figure of a body in between them. Her face was hot and her body felt glowing. She stared hard at the body between her legs. It was Jo; she was looking up at Zara with a smile on her wet lips.

"I just wanted you to have some of the pleasures I had on the ferry and awaken that part of you that's been asleep too long."

Zara did feel awakened and had enjoyed this new experience. What so amazed her was that she did not feel in the least embarrassed; there had always been a sexual undercurrent flowing between her and Jo that had lain dormant for too long. Jo was definitely creating a 'new' Zara, and she was beginning to like it.

Jo came up towards Zara and lay on her shoulder. Zara entwined her fingertips in Jo's curls and stroked her head. They lay like this for a while, just simply enjoying each other's company and eventually drifting back to sleep again.

This time it was Zara who woke first. She felt hungry and remembered that they had not eaten since the coach stopped for a snack at the café all those hours ago. The clock on the wall showed 8.45pm. 'No wonder I'm hungry,' she thought and turned to look at Jo asleep on her breast. She was discovering things about Jo and about herself that she would never have imagined possible. Zara stroked Jo's hair and kissed her forehead. "Time to wake up, sweetie. It's time for dinner."

Jo stirred, sensually rubbing her naked body against Zara's.

Zara gently stroked and shook Jo's shoulder and said, a little louder this time, "Jo, food. Time to get up."

This had the required effect and Jo awoke, looked at Zara's face, slowly tilted her head up and placed her warm sleepy mouth onto Zara's lips. She kissed Zara with her tongue roaming over her teeth and around her mouth and then she pulled away saying, "That'll have to do, I'm starving. Let's find a restaurant near here and then join the nightlife."

Zara laughed and threw a pillow at Jo, "You're a little tease, one of these days someone will tease you and I want to be there to watch your reaction."

CHAPTER FOUR

Zara gazed out of the window of the little café and sipped the last dregs of her coffee; she watched the street outside preparing for the night ahead. The tables and chairs had been transformed by the waiters into relaxing romantic seating by adding cushions to the chairs and candles to the tables. 'I wonder if I will see Noel again or do I put it down to yet another experience,' Zara thought.

Jo broke the silence and said, "I wonder if the rest of the coach passengers are enjoying their 'Red Light' tour."

Zara placed the cup back into its saucer and absent mindedly played with the sugar tongs, thinking, 'I wish I had been more assertive and told him where we were staying. I must be more active and not let opportunities pass me by.'

"Zara, I said, 'I wonder if the rest of the passengers are enjoying their tour.' Can you hear me? Hello, is there anybody in there?" Jo's voice grew louder.

Zara heard this remark and realised that she had been ignoring her friend. "Sorry Jo. I was just thinking about that nice gentleman that I met on the ferry. He was so considerate, and I wish there were more like him around."

"There are; they're just waiting out there for you to find them and you're not going to do that sitting here moping. Come on, let's pay the bill and find some night life." Jo got up from the table, put the money for the meal in the salver provided, "I'll pay for this, you can buy the drinks at the next place. Grab your jacket; we're going to hit the town."

They found a night club tucked down a side street which they only spotted because it had a large neon pineapple above its door. 'L' Ananas' was a suggested place for night life, offered in the tour guide that Jo had received with her tickets. It said in the guide that it was open until late, fairly inexpensive and the music was 'modern'. Jo wondered when the tour guide had been printed and what it classed as modern, but they decided that it was wise to go somewhere recommended on their first night. Inside it was welcoming and full of tourists. The bar sold many English beers and there were signs stating that they all spoke English.

"We'll not find any Frenchies here," Jo said with regret, remembering her pleasant experience with the French man on the ferry.

Zara looked around and agreed, though it definitely felt comfortable to her. The lighting was warm and friendly, the tables were lit by small lanterns and it didn't have the stale sweaty smell that some night clubs had. It wasn't too far from their hotel either, just three stops on the Metro.

"It'll be nice just the two of us, a girl's night out. Let's just enjoy the music and have a little fun," Zara said feeling rather grateful for finding such a calm place after her experiences so far.

"Oh Zara! You're taking the lead here are you?" Jo teased. "Take it away girl, I'm right behind you; lead on."

Zara laughed. "Don't you know it," she said as she led them to the dance floor. They danced together for most of the night, stopping to refill their glasses occasionally. Zara noticed Jo viewing the talent and hoped that she would not find anything suitable here; she was quite happy with a girl's night out, just enjoying her friend's company.

During one of the later songs of the evening, two men tried to dance in between them and split them up. Zara felt nervous, she did not want this tonight; she hoped Jo was feeling the same way. She need not have worried as Jo said very loudly, "We're together, get it? We're an item," and she moved towards Zara and started a sexual dance that involved Jo sliding her body up and down Zara's.

The men watched and were enthralled; they did not move on to other more possible women, which Zara had expected, but they stood and watched Jo's erotic exhibition and obviously enjoyed the entertainment.

Zara could see Jo was aware that she was on exhibition and was in her element; she had an audience and wasn't about to quit. She gyrated her body up and down Zara, using every opportunity to touch her intimately.

Zara giggled, Jo was a born tease. They could see the men were getting excited by Jo's actions and Zara felt the stirrings of her own sexuality; she joined Jo in the fun and twisted her body in and around Jo's movements. Together they gave a dance that deserved to be in the 'Moulin Rouge' and not in 'L' Ananas'.

Other dancers were watching them too and the next they knew it the DJ was speaking over his microphone, "Well look what we have here tonight, our very own floor show, ladies and gentlemen. Take it away girls." When the record finished the DJ asked everyone to give them a round of applause and thanked them for the show by offering them each a free drink at the bar. Jo smiled and thanked the DJ and headed to the bar to collect her reward. Zara followed, feeling herself glow with the praise; she was amazed that she was quite enjoying the attention.

At the bar the two men, that had been the reason for the exhibition, joined them and introduced themselves as Karl and Ryan. A friend of theirs was getting married soon and they were two of a group of ten; the bet for the night had been to split into pairs and report back at the end of the evening, at which point it would be decided the two that had the biggest experience would win the bet. Karl and Ryan admitted that they just wanted a night out and were not bothered about the bet; they would leave that to the more adventurous of the group.

"That was quite a spectacle you two just gave. Are you professional dancers?" Ryan asked.

"Yes, but we're on holiday and it was just a bit of fun," Jo replied, the lies tripping so easily off of her tongue as she looked towards Zara, her eyes laughing. "This is Lou and I'm Suzy," she introduced herself and Zara. "I'm sorry I was so rude to you on the dance floor, I hope I didn't offend you, it's just that we wanted to dance alone tonight," Jo purred looking straight into Ryan's eyes and getting the response she had hoped for. The man's eyes widened and his pupils dilated showing the lustful response that Jo had triggered.

Zara watched Jo as her charm switched on and both Ryan and Karl were caught in her web. 'She reminds me of a black widow spider,' Zara thought. 'Ensnaring her victims for the night, and preparing them for their eventual torture and death.'

The DJ crooned that it was smooch time, so these were going to be the last two records of the evening. He advised everybody grab a partner to say a romantic goodnight to.

"Would you like to dance?" Ryan asked Jo.

"If Lou has no objections," Jo said looking at Zara.

For a moment Zara did not know who she was talking about but then caught on and played along with her. "No of course I don't mind, Suzy, you go right ahead," Zara said enjoying following Jo's story and felt even a little naughty in doing so.

Ryan led Jo onto the dance floor and wrapped his arms around her waist, pulling her closer to him. Zara could see Jo's face over Ryan's shoulder and received a cheeky wink from her. Taking this as an instruction, she turned to Karl, "Shall we?" Zara asked, giving him some encouragement.

"Oh yes," he replied huskily and they too joined the rest of the dancers on the floor.

The four of them smooched the first record away. Zara could see Ryan stroking his hands down Jo's back and onto her backside, cupping her cheeks in the palms of his hands; she saw Jo tease him in return with a thrust of her hips towards his. She could also feel her own partner getting excited and gave him encouragement by pushing her own pelvis into his groin copying Jo's movements.

Jo winked again at Zara and made signals of partner swopping for the second record. Zara started to steer Karl towards Jo and Ryan and as the next record started to run onto the last, Jo and Zara swopped partners, leaving the men watching amazed at their unbelievable luck.

The music continued and Zara could feel the heat from her partner as he leant forward and started to nuzzle her with his lips. Zara leant her head back to expose her neck to his advances; his lips travelled under her chin and to her left ear where he nipped the skin underneath it with his teeth. Zara felt her body's response, as a tingle from her neck right down towards her inner thighs, and showed her appreciation by whispering a sigh in his ear.

Ryan held her close to him and as the music stopped, he kissed her full on the mouth with his tongue hungrily searching for hers. She could smell his male musk of arousal now and found herself excited by this aroma. Zara returned the kiss, tickling his lips with the tip of her tongue; she was enjoying being a tease and could understand the thrill that Jo must receive from her teasing ways.

It was Zara that eventually broke the kiss, explaining that she was going to powder her nose and, touching her fingers to his lips, turned and walked towards the ladies.

Jo followed Zara off the dance floor and joined her in the ladies. They looked at each other and burst out laughing.

"They're both caught in your web, you wicked spider. Are we going to eat them tonight?" Zara asked Jo.

"I don't really fancy either of them; I thought that they were a little dull, shall we make an escape?" Jo said pointing to the open window.

Zara looked at the window and then at Jo and realised that she was serious. Zara was not sure that this was the wisest thing to do; they did not really know Paris well enough to go gallivanting into the night. But she remembered what Jo had said earlier that day about having *fun*. 'What the hell,' she thought. 'This is supposed to be an exciting holiday after all.'

Jo gave Zara a leg up to the window and she pulled herself through, followed by Jo climbing onto the sink and heaving her own body through.

Outside was a small back alley on the opposite side of the entrance, so they made a clean escape and ran out into the street laughing.

They caught the Metro back to their hotel, giggling the whole time like naughty school girls, and entered their bedroom breathless as though back from their first double-date.

"Well what did you think of your first night in Paris?" Jo asked Zara.

"I loved it Jo. I'm really glad you asked me to come with you. I am definitely unwinding and haven't once thought about work. What 'fun' have you planned for us for tomorrow?"

"I don't plan anything; it all just seems to happen; that's what fun is all about. Planning things brings routine and that brings boredom. Remember that Zara," Jo said in the tone of a big sister.

CHAPTER FIVE

"There it is" Zara pointed to a street on the map. 'Rue du Faulbourg St. Honore'. That's where the tour guide said the boutiques are." Jo looked over Zara's shoulder at the map.

On the Sunday, they had joined the other coach passengers on a trip to Versailles to see the palace and its famous Hall of Mirrors, which marvelled them both. Now they were both sick of the coach, its humdrum passengers, and stayed attractions; they wanted to see Paris on their feet. They were sitting on a bench in Camps de Mars near to the Eiffel Tower. They had 'done' the Eiffel Tower that morning on a tour and had decided a shopping trip for the afternoon away from the coach was called for.

Zara dunked her croissant in her coffee, copying the French people she had seen that morning at breakfast in the hotel. "It isn't very far away, only four stops on the Metro. I think while we're buying our tickets, we should see if they do a cheap week pass like the London underground does. It would save us some money."

"You are so efficient Zara; I'd be lost without you. Together we're a great team: you do the organising and I add the fun," Jo said and received a bash on the arm from the map book that Zara was holding.

"You cheeky thing, I can provide fun too. I'm not just the efficient organiser you know," Zara said, feeling a little hurt by Jo's remark.

So far it really had been Jo that had provided the fun, but Zara felt this rubbing off on her and was going to prove to Jo that she too could take the lead to produce some exhilarating adventures for them.

Jo put her empty coffee cup in the bin and stretched her legs out in front of her. "Isn't the sun gorgeous, I could sit here all day, just basking in the heat. Do we have to go to the shops?" Jo asked shutting her eyes whilst she soaked up the sun's rays.

"Yes. How am I going to make a new image of myself if I don't have any new clothes? Come on you lazy thing, let's get going," Zara responded decisively as she pulled Jo up from the bench.

They spent the afternoon walking up and down the fashion shops, nipping in and out and trying on different items of clothing. Zara felt like she was sixteen again and remembered the hours that she had spent in 'Next' just looking for the right pair of pants.

In a shoe shop, Jo had the female assistant in a fluster trying to understand exactly what Jo required. Jo did not help the poor girl by using pidgin English and a cockney accent with using cockney rhyming slang as well, made her job even harder.

"I need something for me plates of meat, what have you got luv?"

"Pardon mademoiselle?" the girl replied looking worried.

"Me plates of meat luv," Jo said again and pointed to her feet

"Je non comprendre pas mademoiselle," was the sweet girl's reply, trying very hard to understand. "Cen'est pas une boucherie."

Jo shrugged her shoulders, huffed and walked out of the shop with Zara following guiltily behind her.

"That was wicked Jo, you ought to be ashamed of yourself. That poor girl," Zara said as they cleared the shop.

Jo was laughing and turned to Zara saying, "I don't understand miss, this is not a butcher's shop. Come on Zara you've got to laugh, it was only a bit of fun."

Zara looked at Jo and smiled. She was right, it was only a bit of fun; they had not persisted in humiliating the girl. But still, Zara couldn't help but think it was a bit of mean spirited fun, even if it was harmless. Zara linked arms with Jo and gave her a squeeze, "What shall we do next?"

They walked on down the street and stopped outside a very classy boutique. They looked through the window into the small boutique. It was elaborately decorated in different shades of purple and all the metal fittings were gold-coloured, including the dress rails and hangers. There was no one in the shop but a solitary distinguished man in his early thirties, dressed in a suit and cufflinks. He seemed far too classy to be working in a boutique; Zara imagined he must be the owner and maybe even a famous fashion designer.

"Look at him Zara, he looks bored; shall we go and make his day?" Jo asked nodding in the direction of the man.

Zara looked closer at him and thought that he was the epitome of the French male archetype. He had dark sultry looks with an olive complexion to match and was quite attractive in a moody sort of way. "Yes let's," Zara answered Jo's question.

They both entered the shop and started to browse around the expensive clothes.

"You are both beautiful English roses, 1 can tell by the way you move. Can I help you Mademoiselles?" he asked them in his sexy French accent.

"Thank you sir, but we are just looking," Jo replied with as much grace as she could muster without bursting into giggles.

Zara watched as the man smiled and nodded, and returned to his desk to busy himself with some labels. He was definitely good looking, she decided. He was about six feet tall with an excellent body in a suit that was cut to fit him perfectly. She walked towards Jo and in a hushed voice said, "Mmm, he's nice isn't he?"

Jo raised her eyebrows and smirked at Zara's comment and then they both returned to browsing through the stock. They were looking along a rail when Jo found something and pulled it out for Zara to see. Jo had chosen a low cut, scarlet dress with a silken laced back and was holding it out for Zara.

"I can't wear that, it would hardly cover me," Zara exclaimed when Jo asked her to try it on.

"The colour will suit you down to the ground and what did I say about showing off your delicious body?" Jo thrust the dress into Zara's hands and pointed her to the dressing room, go in there and let me see you when you've got it on. Go on," she said giving Zara a gentle push in the direction of the dressing room.

Behind the curtains Zara undressed, slid the flimsy fabric over her shoulders and watched the dress softly fall down over her body. It was so light as it was made of a silken mesh with silk laces covering her back and very little covering her front. The hem line was around her ankles and Zara let her eyes travel up from the hem to the mirror; she could see her bra was showing so with a simple movement on her strap, she removed the bra.

Zara readjusted the dress and again looked in the mirror; her eyes were drawn to her cleavage. The dark shadow of the groove between her breasts was highlighted by the scarlet colour of the dress. Jo had been right, Zara certainly liked what she saw, and she thought, 'Jo's right I ought to show my body off more.'

Her breasts were full and firm; they filled the low cut perfectly and she could see the soft projection of her nipples through the fine fabric. Zara ran her fingers over the fabric and felt the soft curves of her waistline to her hips. She felt sexy. 'I wonder,' Zara thought. She drew the curtain to one side and stepped out into the shop.

Jo was waiting and gave Zara a very appreciative eye.

Zara was thinking fast now, right little miss, two can play teasing games. She walked seductively towards Jo and stopped directly in front of her.

"Do you like what you see?" she asked as she reached down to Jo's hand and lifted it up to her mouth. Zara's tongue touched Jo's fingers and she trailed it down one finger and up the next, looking Jo directly in the eyes as she did so.

Jo's pupils had started to dilate and Zara watched as her mouth parted in an expectant need. 'She wants me,' Zara thought. 'I *can* tease, just like she does. I wonder what she thinks to that.' She dropped Jo's hand and smiled, turned around and walked slowly back to the dressing room.

Back in the cubicle, Zara peeped through the curtain and saw Jo's reaction. 'Yes madam,' she thought. 'It's about time you had a bit of your own medicine. I hold power too and I hadn't realised how much until now.'

Jo looked flustered and was making a big pretence of finding something interesting on a rail to hide her discomfort. From her peephole, Zara could also see the male shop assistant. He was staring at Jo.

He must have seen the whole episode, Zara thought and she watched as he left his desk and walked towards Jo, placed a hand on her shoulder and whispered something in her ear. Jo looked up at him and nodded; Zara watched Jo head for the cubicle next to her own and the man turn the sign to 'ferme', lock the door and join Jo in the cubicle.

Zara moved her position and adjusting the curtain, found a new peephole, in the curtain dividing the two cubicles. The man was kissing Jo's face and neck whilst pushing her skirt up to her hips; Jo's head was tilted back and Zara saw the man's tongue trace a line down Jo's neck to her shoulder, pulling her shoulder strap down with his teeth in the process. Jo was wriggling and Zara saw she was rolling a condom on to the man's erection. Zara watched as the man pushed Jo's legs apart and made an upward thrust; Jo made a stifled groan as the man covered her mouth with his to prevent any more noise. Their bodies were pressed so closely to each other. Zara watched as they both shifted slightly with Jo raising one leg and supported it on the chair in the cubicle. By now the man had pulled Jo's shoulder strap down completely exposing one breast; his mouth teased her nipple with gentle kisses and nips.

Zara found herself aroused by their excitement and her own act of voyeurism; she removed the scarlet dress and stood naked, but for her high heeled shoes. She ran her hands down between her thighs and let her fingers wander over the wetness of her lips. Starting a rhythmic massage on her clitoris, she proceeded to satiate her arousal. Leaning forward, she returned to her peephole and saw Jo's face now in ecstasy; her head bent back as her body arced. Zara's own fingers continued their work whilst with her other hand she pulled the curtain slightly to one side.

Her own arousal would not let her be apart from this and she leant forward some more and kissed Jo's lips. Jo opened her eyes and saw Zara; the man looked up and saw Zara also, his dark eyes were watching her. Jo started to moan again and this time Zara covered her mouth and entwined her tongue with her own. Zara could feel the start of her orgasm and pressed her fingers deeply inside herself as the first ripple overtook her. Zara took each breath from Jo's mouth as she felt Jo's mouth shiver with each pulse of her own orgasm.

The man was close to his release also as he watched Zara and Jo. Seeing their tongues entwined he gave one last thrust and felt his own climax start to pump through him. Zara felt Jo again react to the stimulus inside of her now and she sucked on Zara's tongue as she again reached orgasm.

Zara moved gently away from Jo's mouth and drew back into her own cubicle. Back inside she smiled as she thought of the fun that she had instigated. She started to dress again and could hear the pair of them rearranging their clothes in the cubicle next to her, talking in hushed tones.

Zara left her cubicle with a warm glow inside; behind her followed the shop assistant and Jo.

The shop assistant packed the dress into a box and pressed the till keys, the Zeros showed up clearly and the shop assistant smiled and said, "Merci beucoup Mademoiselles." As he opened the door to let them out; Jo and Zara smiled and said thank you also, then waved as they left the shop.

The Metro was dark after the brightness of the afternoon sunshine and Jo and Zara sat quietly next to each other; the box that held the scarlet dress was laid across their knees.

Zara had never known Jo to be so quiet; she had hardly said a word since they had left the boutique. Zara was worried, a subtle change was noticeable in their relationship and she hoped that she had not ruined it.

Jo broke the silence, "Shall we get off at the next stop and walk along the Seine for a while, it's such a lovely day and it would be a shame to miss it," Jo said looking at the underground map above their heads. "Which is our next stop, Zara? I don't understand these maps."

Zara looked at Jo's confused expression and smiled, "You little lost thing you. This one, 'St. Michel', that's close to where all the artists sit painting pictures, just waiting to be noticed by a passing art collector and become famous one day." Zara pointed to the stop on the map.

"Right, let's get off here and see a bit of culture then." Jo pulled herself up and held out a hand to help her friend up. Zara took Jo's hand with her free one, whilst in her other hand she held the box that had balanced their standing in the relationship, along with her beautiful new red dress.

Back outside in the sunshine with the box underneath one of Zara's arms and Jo linked in the other, the women strolled along the water's edge, watching the cruise boats pass by filled with tourists pointing at the ancient buildings. High above their heads were little window boxes overflowing with summer flowers and bright blue sun blinds jutting out over the window tops. There was the smell of freshly percolated coffee mixed with oil paints and turpentine. The atmosphere of the place, made Zara, feel quite light-headed and extremely comfortable.

They walked along viewing different artists' works as they passed by. They stopped at a brasserie halfway up a steep narrow street and sat outside at a metal table with a parasol over their heads, drinking their titchy cups of espresso.

"I feel like I'm in an advert for a French car waiting for 'Papa' to arrive'," Jo said gazing up the street at an artist busy cleaning his brushes with an old rag.

"The artists don't look all that French, do they? They look like poor university students trying to earn a living to pay for their book lists to me," Zara said watching the artist also. He picked up his palette and squirted some paint, which he then agitated with his finger in slow, circular movements, mixing the colour with the white already on the palette.

"Christ! That is so sexy," Jo said huskily. "That man is turning me on; just watch his finger's movements Zara."

'You're insatiable,' Zara chided, but she too was mesmerised by the artist's movements. They watched as the artist softly rotated his finger over the oily paint.

"Why doesn't he use a spatula like the other artists? He'll get covered in the stuff doing it like that." Jo could not take her eyes off of his hands.

They both watched the artist finish mixing the paint and start to smudge the paint onto the canvas, still using his fingers.

"I think he's after a special texture on his painting. It looks like he's painting those geraniums opposite him in that doorway," Zara pointed to a small wooden door with three stone steps leading up to it. On the steps were several metal pots, stacked with brightly coloured flowers.

"I'm going to go and watch him for a while, it's so peaceful here after the rush and bustle of the shops." Jo got up and walked up to the street towards the man, crouched down beside him and looked at the canvas.

Zara watched Jo for a while, thinking that she never ceased to amaze her. One minute she was playing the fool and the next she was quiet and serene. 'She's right,' Zara thought. 'It is so peaceful here.' She leaned back in her chair and closed her eyes enjoying the warm sun upon her face and listening to the soft sounds around her: a quiet conversation from an elderly couple sitting at a table nearby, the espresso machine gushing from inside the small brasserie, the slow chug from a barge travelling slowly down the river Seine. She could smell the strong scent of the geraniums that seemed to be decorating every doorway and windowsill in this part of the city. She was so glad she had chosen to come with Jo on the holiday; she had forgotten how it felt to relax so completely.

When she eventually opened her eyes she saw Jo deep in conversation with the artist. It looked as though Jo was asking the artist something. Zara could not hear what she was saying, nor the reply, but saw the artist smile and nod. Zara, intrigued, picked up the box and walked up the street towards the two of them; she was not about to miss out on any 'fun' that Jo was obviously having. She knew Jo was not seriously interested in what the artist was painting but more in the way that he was painting it.

"He paints people as well as flowers," Jo said to Zara as she reached them. "He says he is only painting this to pass the time. He also speaks very good English," Jo smiled her praise at the artist's face and received a smile in return.

'She's off again,' thought Zara. 'What a flirt.'

"Do you paint for a living or as a hobby?" Zara asked the artist.

"I paint because I have a love for it. If it pays I eat, if no…," he shrugged his shoulders as he replied to Zara.

"…You don't," Zara finished his sentence for him. "Oh, that's a true artist speaking." Zara laughed inwardly. 'This man is not for real,' she thought.

"You are both beautiful women. I would like to paint you. You would sell and I would eat, yes?" The artist smiled and his eyes travelled over their bodies as he spoke.

"Yes," Jo said quickly, her face flushing slightly with desire under his gaze. "That would be lovely, wouldn't it Zara? I can just see us in oils, can't you?"

The artist looked up at the sun that was slowly setting, "Come, the light is going now. I will take you to my studio. I have light all of the night there. Follow me, please." He picked up his painting case, palette and canvas and walked towards the wooden door behind the geraniums that he had been painting.

Zara watched him as he moved towards the door; his movements were almost graceful, like a dancer's.

"This way, you come," he said, turning to face them and gesturing to his front door.

Zara looked at Jo as she trotted after him. 'What have you gotten us into now? Yet another 'new' experience I expect,' she thought to herself as she made a move to follow them up the steps.

CHAPTER SIX

The door led straight into a kitchen, well that is what Zara thought it was. Apart from a microwave, a coffee percolator and a sink though, there was little else to show that it was a kitchen. The walls were covered in pictorial silks, depicting scenes of the countryside. There was a large one above a seat consisting of farmyard animals, another of a field of poppies and behind Jo there was a circular piece of silk in the shape of a pond with all its insect life. 'This man is definitely not real,' Zara thought. 'Why can't we meet an ordinary man...like Noel?' Zara's thoughts were pulled back to a dance floor and a man's touch that had left a lasting impression on her. It seemed like a thousand days ago now, perhaps even a thousand years and yet even as she thought this, she also thought that it felt like it had only just happened.

After all that had happened to the women so far and all that they had been through, Zara found herself still thinking about Noel. She wondered what he was doing now, and mused he certainly would not be in a kitchen. But then the old Zara reared her ugly head and she thought, he was more likely to be in some model's bed. Zara sighed.

"You like my room?" the artist asked Zara, responding to her sigh as though he thought it was given out of amazement of his kitchen. "You will see my studio, that is good."

"How do you manage to eat with all these animals watching you?" Zara asked him, gesturing with her arm towards the farmyard silk.

"I like to feel close to the natural world," the artist replied, picking up a bottle of red wine from the table and pouring it into two large tall stemmed glasses. "Here, drink and return to nature with me."

Jo and Zara took the proffered drinks and sipped the wine. It was sweet and left warmth on the tongue, down the throat and in the stomach. Jo was smiling and gave Zara a wink and pointed to the glass. Zara frowned not understanding what Jo was trying to tell her. Jo mouthed the word 'strong', and took a large mouthful finishing her drink. Zara looked into her glass and sniffed it, there was nothing different about it except the taste, so she followed Jo's example and emptied her glass too.

The artist was putting his paint case into a large wooden box that doubled as a seat. It had been carved roughly, and had faces of owls poking out around its sides. The man had weird tastes in décor but all of the unusual items were definitely creative and artistic.

Zara watched him; his hands and fingers moved slowly, taking their time to finish each action properly and carefully. He was closing the latch on the box and this simple action kept Zara and Jo entranced. His long, ochre coloured hair fell over his face and revealed part of a tattoo on the back of his neck. He was wearing a tie-dyed t-shirt that was too large for his slim frame, and loose cotton trousers.

He stood up and smiled again at the two of them. "Come," he said and opened a door to their left.

Jo picked up the bottle of wine and followed him, taking Zara by the arm and leading her. They walked along a dark hall and down some stone steps. The air felt cold and reminded Zara of her parents' cellar steps. The artist opened a door at the bottom of the steps and released a burst of light and warmth.

"This is my studio," the artist stepped to one side to let them pass. They walked into a warm, unusually lit room that was empty but for a large groundsheet covering the floor, a collection of tins and buckets lined up against one wall and an empty canvas on the other. The lights were placed at different angles on the ceiling and walls, resulting in a soft pool of light in the centre of the room, like a soft spotlight on a stage. "Wow! You work in here?" Jo asked incredulously.

"When I am able and tonight I am able as you will be painted," he replied in a soft voice, walking over to the collection of tins. "First I will choose the colours." The artist started to take the lids off of some of the tins and put several to one side.

Zara whispered to Jo, "What have you gotten us into, maybe we should go while we still can."

Jo shook her head and whispered back, "He's harmless and anyway I think he's cute." She turned to the artist and asked, "Where and how do you want us to pose?"

"You do not 'pose' for me, this is natural art. You simply be you, and I will paint. Yes?"

"Yes," was all Jo could think of replying.

Zara leant to Jo's ear again "He's one of those fringe artists isn't he, like the ones you see at the Edinburgh Festival; we'll probably end up being pickled in formaldehyde. Come on let's go," Zara pulled Jo towards the door but was stopped by the artist who reached it before her.

"Do not worry, I am a peaceful person. I just paint and love. You are both beautiful women, I show the art world your beauty. Now please, feel comfortable. Have more wine, there is plenty. I will paint." They stood watching as he refilled their glasses and returned to his tins.

Zara was starting to feel warm and happy, this wine was the cause, she was sure of that. The alcohol content was definitely high. Zara looked at Jo who was finishing her second glass and pouring another. Zara watched her friend and thought that she was moving very slowly as she took another mouthful of wine from her own glass.

"I feel so warm in here, I need to cool down," Jo said removing some of her clothing. "Phew, I feel kind of warm and sleepy." Her clothes came off slowly like she was peeling an onion, removing everything but her underwear.

"That is good," said the artist. "It will be natural." He walked to the central pool of light carrying two large buckets and an open tin; he emptied the buckets' contents onto the floor, out tumbled thousands of feathers, hovering in the air, before floating gently down to cover the groundsheet.

Zara watched; was she dreaming this? She started to feel very warm and capricious and, like Jo, felt the warmth and need to remove her clothes. Zara undressed slowly removing her clothes and dropping them where she stood. Soon both women were left standing in their underwear.

The artist reached into the tin and drew out some pale blue silk. The piece of material trailed after him along the feathered floor as he walked towards Jo and tied the end that he was holding to her wrist. While he did this, he stroked Jo's shoulder and kissed her neck. Then he turned to face Zara.

The artist raised his t-shirt and pulled it over his head, letting it fall to the floor. His chest and nipples were exposed and his nipples were pierced; through each nipple was a small silver ring. Zara stood entranced by his slim sinewy body. She then walked around him trailing her fingers over his skin, relishing in the feel of each delicate muscle so lean and sleek; and his back, now bare, revealed a tattoo. It was a torrent of water, a waterfall, running from under his long hair down his spine and disappearing behind his trousers.

Zara, in the alcohol-induced dream, raised her hand up to move his hair to one side to get a full view of the tattoo. With it now exposed, Zara traced her fingertips over the water from his neck to the top of his trousers.

The artist reached an arm behind him and grasped Zara's arm gently, moving her round to stand next to Jo. He then raised Zara's hand up to his lips and kissed her fingers, running his tongue up her arm, over her shoulder and across the top of her breasts. His tongue then travelled down her stomach and kneeling down in front of her, he tied the silk material to her ankle. His tongue's action did not feel sexual to Zara, instead she felt as if she had just been tasted and was a delicacy at a banquet.

Zara looked down at his bent back as he tied the silk around her ankle and proceeded to run his tongue over her foot and between her toes, she reached out again to touch the waterfall and her fingers entwined themselves in his hair as she felt its heavy silkiness.

The artist lifted his head and he looked up at her," I will paint you both with silk and feathers. You like?"

Zara nodded, this was all so unreal, but it felt beautiful, and so relaxed. She let go of his hair, letting the silkiness run through her fingers, and trailed her fingers down his nose and to his mouth.

"I like," she said huskily, hardly daring to speak lest she break the spell.

Jo knelt down, facing the artist and took Zara's hand from his mouth. She kissed it gently, wrapping the silk tie around her arm, shortening its length and drawing Zara's leg nearer to her. Zara felt her body tremble and her knees quiver as Jo's fingers made circular motions at the back of her knee and she slowly lowered herself to join Jo amongst the feathers.

The artist stood up and walked to collect his paints and over to the canvas where he prepared to paint.

"Not yet please," Jo's voice softly broke the silence.

The artist walked back and again joined them on the floor. He took Jo's face gently in his hands, stroking her cheeks with his fingers and said, "The time is right, I must mon cherie." One of his hands left Jo's face and he placed it on Zara's cheek. "You have each other, it is natural, just be beautiful together."

Zara looked into his eyes and her heart melted; he was so beautiful, so gentle. She watched him lean across the feathered floor and reach for their glasses, he took a mouthful from one and bringing Zara and Jo's faces to his, kissed them both, releasing some warm wine into their mouths as he did so. With his proficient hands, he tipped some wine into each of their mouths and gently turned their faces and lips to each other.

Whilst Zara and Jo were kissing the artist returned to his canvas and proceeded to paint. He watched them as he painted and painted what he saw: red mouths sealed in a kiss, red wine trickling down necks and onto shoulders, bodies entwined with legs wrapped around each other, arms holding backs and waists in an embrace of love, hair a mixture of black sleek strands and brown curly locks, contrasting skin tones with Zara's olive complexion entwined with Jo's creamy white all with a dash of pale blue silk running between. And the beautifully natural and artistic dance captured in a pool of soft light on a bed of feathers.

The women fell into a serene deep sleep, still in a full embrace, and the artist worked on through the night and into the dawn.

CHAPTER SEVEN

The smell of freshly percolated coffee reached Zara's nostrils and she relished the smell, breathing deeply. She turned her head smiling at the thought of fresh coffee. Her head ached, though. She raised a hand up to massage her temples and moved the sheet that was covering her. That's when she opened her eyes and saw Jo's curly hair. Jo was lying with her back to Zara; they were snuggled spooning together, on the floor, but not in the hotel. The room smelt strongly of oils and turpentine, reminding Zara of school art classes.

"Jo, wake up its morning..." Zara looked around the dimly lit room with no natural light. "At least, I think it is."

Jo stirred and groaned, "Christ my head hurts, I must have drunk too much wine last night. Oh, last night. Was it real or was it a dream? Can you remember any of it Zara?" Jo asked turning over to face her friend.

"I just remember feeling loved. It was beautiful," Zara let out a soft satisfied hum and lay on her back and stretched like an awakening cat.

The lights on the ceiling had been dimmed. Zara could feel the feathers and enjoyed their softness between her fingers. The night's events came vaguely back to her and a warm feeling glowed through her;

she may have a terrible hangover, but she felt so good inside.

Jo sat up and looked down at Zara. "You look like the cat that's had the cream," she said. "And I don't think there was even any sex. That was a powerful bottle of wine."

Zara smiled contentedly back, looked around the room again and wondered where the artist was. She looked at Jo and said, "Do you realise, we never even asked his name?"

The room was shadowed and dim and all that could be seen were the shapes of tins and buckets. The door opened and the artist walked in carrying two mugs of coffee. "Good Morning. You are awake. I hear your voices from above."

He bent down and handed Jo her coffee. Zara noticed that his long, silken hair was now bound in a yellow bandanna and he had swapped his t-shirt for a creamy muslin shirt which was thin enough to reveal his pierced nipples through the fabric.

As he leant to pass her coffee over, she could smell that he had recently showered and he smelt of ylang-ylang flowers. "What time is it?" Zara asked.

"It is time to eat. I will fetch some croissants and while I am gone you may both freshen up. There is a shower upstairs, please help yourselves." He left them to return upstairs.

"My head aches so much I think I'll pass on that and go back to the hotel to freshen up and have a proper sleep." Jo started to dress herself, "Are you coming?"

"We can't just leave him, anyway we haven't seen the painting yet. I fancy staying here for a while, it's so peaceful. You can go back and I'll join you later." Zara did not want to leave this tranquil place, it had been a long time since she had felt so at peace; and her head only hurt if she moved it quickly.

"You sure you'll be alright? You were frightened of being pickled last night," Jo laughed and then grimaced in pain. "This head needs an aspirin and a sleep in a bed. I'm off," she bent down and kissed Zara goodbye wishing her good luck . Jo disappeared leaving Zara feeling strange, comfortable yet strange. 'That was a quick departure,' thought Zara picking up her clothes and walking, naked, to find the shower room.

She walked up the steps, along the dark hall and back into the kitchen.

'Where could the shower be?' she wondered, looking around the room for another exit. There were no more doors but there was a long silk that covered a doorway. She pulled it to one side and walked through to another set of stairs. The stairs took her up to a large room with bare, polished floorboards that reflected the sunshine pouring through the large skylight in the ceiling. There was a pile of quilted fabrics on the floor and several cushions. 'What a beautiful homemade bed,' she thought and continued her search for the shower.

The shower was not in a room on its own, it was tucked into the corner of the bedroom with a coloured stained glass panel that strew colours all across the floor from the sun's rays that were blasting through the window in the ceiling.

Zara dropped her clothes onto the floor, turned on the shower and stepped in. The warm water ran over her hair and body and she stood with her face upturned to the shower-head, letting the water cascade down over her nakedness. It felt so gorgeous.

To her right there was a small shelf with tiny phials on it. She looked along them, and opened and sniffed one or two. They were perfumed oils. Zara chose the Patchouli and let a few drops loose on to a sponge. She cleansed and perfumed herself with the sponge, smoothing it all over her body.

She turned the shower off and stepped out onto the mat. She could not see any towels but found a large piece of muslin next to the shower. 'I hope this is his towel,' she thought as she wrapped it around her. The material quickly absorbed the water from her body and left her standing in a sun beam of colours looking like a patch of oil floating on the water.

"A living spectrum of light. My mind's eye has taken a photo so I can paint this," the artist said standing looking at her. He placed the bag of croissants down on a small wooden table and walked over to stand in front of her. "You are so beautiful; you fill my head with images to paint and my heart with images to love." He then raised his arm and released the wet muslin from her body; it fell to the floor at her feet.

Zara stood naked in the sunlight with the colours from the glass panel radiating over her skin. The artist stood gazing at, but not touching, Zara's body; his eyes wandered from her toes all over her body until they reached her face.

Zara felt that she was again being tasted but this time it was different, this time she could feel the sexuality in it. The atmosphere was electric. The artist stood staring into Zara's eyes; it felt so powerful that Zara thought she would orgasm without even being touched. She lifted her arm to the artist's bandanna and released his long hair letting it fall around his shoulders. She took a step nearer to him and leant towards his neck where she rested her head, breathing in his aroma.

The artist responded by taking her wet hair in both his hands and twisting it through his fingers, squeezing out droplets of water that Zara could feel run down her back in small rivulets making her skin tingle and her nipples harden in response.

Zara needed to feel this extraordinary man inside her; she wanted him to make love to her completely.

She hadn't had intercourse since Jamaica and her body was crying out for this man and his sensuality.

Zara removed his shirt and let it drop to the floor behind him. He stood there passively letting her take the lead, not wanting to rush her into anything she did not want. As Zara started to kiss his shoulder and chest, he released her hair from his fingers which left her head free to explore him. Zara flicked one of his silver nipple rings with her tongue and then took it between her teeth and pulled gently; the artist's breathing increased and Zara felt his chest move with each breath. Her hands rolled his loose trousers over his hips and down past his thighs, where they fell to the floor releasing his penis, entirely free, to stand erect.

Zara moved downwards to kneel in front of him, brushing her breasts past the tip of his penis on the way. She took his erection in her hands and moved her mouth over its tip, pushing the silky skin back with her lips. The artist's hands returned to Zara's hair and as her mouth worked, his hands toyed with the wet strands. Zara's movements became faster and she could feel him swelling with excitement in her mouth and her tongue tasted the salty tell tale sign that his orgasm was near. The artist then stopped her head by holding her hair more firmly and gently pulling it away from him. She released her mouth's hold and looked up to meet his eyes, he was shaking his head. He pulled her up to him, lifted her off her feet and laid her down on top of the quilts.

"You lay here and I enjoy you. It is now my turn to taste," he said moving her legs apart. The artist lay between her legs and kissed her breasts, this time he did not avoid her nipples. With his ever slow attentive movements he nibbled them, sucking them into his mouth and releasing them again and again until Zara felt that they would burst with the pleasure.

His mouth left her breasts and his fingers took their places, rolling the hard buds between finger and thumb. Then his face snuggled between her thighs and she could feel his silken hair on her skin, sliding and falling down her legs as his face reached her hot, moist opening. 'Don't tease me,' she thought. 'I don't think I can wait any longer.'

He did not tease her; his tongue shot straight into her whilst his mouth surrounded and started to suck. Zara cried out as she felt his tongue rubbing relentlessly on her inside wall that held the secret G-spot. She grasped his head as she climaxed into his mouth and he tasted her pleasure.

Zara had read about Tantric sex and the massaging of the G-spot but had never believed nor experienced it before this.

"You like, yes?" he asked.

"Oh, yes," she replied breathlessly.

Zara sat up and kissed him on the mouth, tasting herself on his lips. She wanted him inside her and again she took control, pushing him gently back onto the quilted fabrics, she straddled his thighs.

He was looking up at her as she guided him into her swollen opening. She stared back into his eyes, as she slowly lowered her body down, feeling his hardness against the sides of her dark wet tunnel. His eyes closed as he moved his hips up to meet her and they joined in a union of passion. Zara felt every thrust deep inside her and became lost in a surreal world again.

She felt the artist's meticulous fingers on her clitoris, and the reactions of a clitoral climax combined the internal orgasm that was overtaking her body. Zara could feel the artist's climax join hers and they reached their peak together in a burst of sensations that rippled through both their bodies.

The croissants were cold by the time the couple got back to them, but Zara was hungry and ate them quickly, licking the pastry off of her fingers so as not to waste any. The artist watched Zara, smiling. She was still naked, sitting up eating croissants with a nameless Frenchman she had just had sex with and it felt good. She had something to tell Jo now, she thought wickedly.

"You were hungry, yes?" he asked.

"I am," Zara said. She felt as though the time she had spent with the long haired Frenchman had been timeless, very much eternal. Without a clock to keep her in the real world, she felt like she had just woken from some mystical power but now that she had re-entered reality again, her stomach had awakened. "So hungry. What time *is* it anyway?"

"The sun says it is late in the afternoon, look," he pointed up to the skylight and Zara could see that the sun was past its peak.

'It must be nearly tea time,' Zara thought. 'Where has the day gone?'

"I must go soon, but first you must show me the painting," Zara requested

"I cannot, it has gone," the artist replied.

Zara looked at him, "What do you mean, gone?" she asked incredulously.

"I took it this morning, while you were sleeping. I have sold it; we eat," he replied simply.

"Sold it. I don't understand, it must have still been wet," Zara could not believe this. Had they slept so long that he had managed to paint their picture, take it away and sell it?

"I have a buyer for my work. I knew that he would buy you, so I painted, I sold and we ate, yes?" the artist replied smiling softly.

"No! We didn't even see it," Zara could feel herself getting angry. How dare he sell it before they had seen it?

The artist held her hand and stroked it saying, "You give me your address and I will send you a photograph." His fingers were caressing Zara's hand slowly and meticulously and his eyes were gazing softly into hers.

How could she be angry with this beautiful man; she leant forward and kissed him on his lips, he responded and she received a sensuous, gentle kiss in return; a kiss goodbye.

CHAPTER EIGHT

"What do you mean, we can't see the painting?" Jo's voice echoed Zara's earlier question to the artist.

Zara was sitting at the mirror giving her long hair a well needed brush, "Don't worry. I've given him my address; he promised that he would send me a photograph of it." Zara replied, looking at Jo's reflection in the mirror.

Zara had been back at the hotel for an hour now and Jo had only just awoken. Zara had spent that hour trying to recall all of the events of the previous 'missing' hours, but the afternoon's sensations were so instilled in her mind that she could not remember much before this.

Jo was sitting in bed, looking back at Zara's face in the mirror. Zara was enjoying seeing Jo flustered for a change. This holiday was rebuilding her sexuality and making her feel more confident to 'let loose', just like Jo had said it would.

"Why did you leave so quickly and not stay for croissants?" Zara asked.

Jo grinned, "I just thought that it was about time you experienced a man again, and you seemed quite taken by him." Jo moved across the bed and leant her chin on Zara's shoulder, looking at their reflection in the mirror. "Well, what was he like?"

Zara pushed Jo's head back and turned around to face her, "Oh, kind of different, in a gentle sort of way."

"Is that it, 'Kind of different'?" Jo asked, starting to dress herself. She giggled, "Did you pull his nipple rings?"

"None of your business," Zara said calmly. "But I'll tell you this; I really need a bit of rough. A dominant man. Someone who takes the lead during sex, you know, a sort of Mr Darcy."

Jo's face changed, her eyes opening wide in surprise. Zara threw her head back laughing at the shocked look on Jo's face and could not miss adding, "I don't mean a man to control my life Jo. I'm firmly in control in my work and social life, but I'm not averse to a bit of male dominance in the bedroom, you know."

Jo laughed, "There I was thinking that I had brought a shrinking violet away with me. Now look at you; you remind me of the Zara I knew in my teens. It's so good to have her back," Jo held Zara's shoulders and pointed her face to the mirror. "Just look at that deep pout, those dilated pupils and the slight flush on the cheeks; you look like you could eat any man alive," Jo leant and whispered in Zara's ear. "Any woman as well, I think."

Zara felt the fine hairs on the back of her neck respond to Jo's husky whisper, but she would not let Jo have her way. She was grateful to Jo for releasing the latent sexuality in her, but it was a man she wanted now; a protective, almost domineering man; one that would give this re-born Zara a run for her money.

"I'm starving; I've only had a few croissants to eat all day," Zara said looking at the clock on the wall. "Shall we have a drink and a bite to eat in the hotel bar and 'mix' with the coach passengers?"

"Why not, I'm hungry too," Jo said heading for their bedroom door. "Come on then. Let's find 'Dick nice but thick', for you to pleasure tonight, shall we?" Jo retorted cheekily as they left their room and headed down the stairs to the hotel bar.

There were only two people in the bar, the old couple who had played backgammon on the coach, who were now sitting looking out the window.

"They think they're still on the coach," Jo whispered to Zara nudging her to look at them.

They walked to the bar and Zara picked up the menu, "It looks like its salad or salad; I don't know what to choose. I think I'll have a salad; what are you having?" Zara passed the menu to Jo.

"There are different types. Oh, look you can have crusty French bread with it; *fancy*. I'm beginning to long for the old fish and chips," Jo said cheekily. As she put the menu down, the gentleman from the old couple came over to the bar.

"You don't have to order luv; you just help yourself from over there," he said, pointing to a buffet table that was stacked with salad foods. "It's free, you know; included in the price. My wife and I have eaten here all week, it saves on the old purse strings you see," he said patting his trouser pocket.

""Thank you. We didn't know," Zara replied gratefully.

"That's all right dear. When you've eaten, come over and have a chat with us. We could do with some different conversation." He left them and returned to his wife.

"Wasn't that nice of him; well come on let's tuck in then," Zara said leading the way to their evening's sustenance.

Zara and Jo piled their salad bowls high. "Go careful on that French dressing Zara, it's the most fattening thing on the salad bar. And you don't want to ruin that figure before you've had a chance to display it in all its glory," Jo said cheekily as she watched Zara trickle some extra oil over her salad, "We've still got two days and two nights left of this holiday."

"Only one useable night left," Zara replied. "We leave quite early on Friday, so I don't think we'll be staying out late Thursday night." It was nearly over Zara thought, the time was flying by and she still hadn't seen Notre-Dame.

"Well we'd better get the guide out and decide what we're going to do during the next two days, before they escape us like today did," Jo said as she walked back to the bar and sat down with her meal.

"Today may have escaped you, but it sure didn't escape me," Zara said as she joined Jo again and sat down laughing. "Where do you fancy going tomorrow?"

Jo frowned and said quietly, "Don't laugh when I tell you this but I need to see Napoleon's Tomb."

"Why should I laugh at that? Anyway what do you mean by 'need to see Napoleon's Tomb'?"

"You will laugh; I know you will; everyone always does." Jo stared at her salad for some time, seemingly conjuring up enough courage to continue. "Alright, here goes. When I was twelve years old, my parents took me to see Napoleon's Tomb; I was flabbergasted by the size of it; you looked down on it from above and when you walked down the stairs to see it close up, it overtook you. It filled the room. I heard someone there tell someone else that Napoleon was so evil that when he died they chopped him up and buried his body in different places so that, if he came back to life, he wouldn't be able to reassemble himself; this amazed me and I asked my mum and dad, *"Is he really in there?"* and I pointed to the tomb. They just laughed at me and carried on walking. So, to this day I still don't know if he is really in there and I want to go again and find out for myself."

Zara burst out laughing, nearly choking on her salad.

"See, I told you, you would laugh, but I'm serious, I still wonder whether he is in there or whether there are bits of him laying about around Paris somewhere," Jo pouted, somewhat deflated.

"You're priceless Jo. I'm sorry if I've upset you by laughing, but I couldn't help it. We will go to Napoleon's tomb tomorrow and we will find out if he's 'really in there'," Zara said, reaching out to Jo's hand and giving it a squeeze to reassure her.

When they had finished their meal they walked over to join the elderly couple, who introduced themselves as George and Edith. Zara and Jo sat chatting to them, swapping stories of what they had seen so far in Paris (making sure they did not tell them the intimate details, of course).

"Thursday is the day I'm really looking forward to," Edith said with a big grin on her face. "I've always wanted to go to Disneyland Paris. It's just a shame the grandchildren are not with us, isn't it George?"

"I'm sure we shall have just as good a time on our own Edie; we still know how to have fun."

Zara watched as George slipped his arm under the table, squeezed Edith's leg and made her jump, and she giggled like a young girl.

"Oh! George, behave yourself," Edith leant forward and said very quietly to Jo. "This Paris air has got to him. He's been very *naughty* here."

"How are you getting to Disneyland?" Jo asked them.

"The coach deary," Edith replied. "You two haven't been around much, so you've missed out on all the trips. The coach is taking us there on Thursday. Why don't you both come along with us?" Edith suggested looking at them enquiringly.

"What a wonderful idea Edith; I've only ever been to Alton Towers. I'll come with you, how about you Zara, are you up for it?" Jo asked.

Zara had never been attracted to America, let alone Disneyland; it was not her idea of fun. She could think of a thousand places that she would rather go to. "I still haven't seen Notre-Dame and I really 'need' to see that." Zara gave great emphasis to the 'need' and received a glower from Jo in return, "You go Jo, I'll spend a cultural day at the cathedral and maybe wander down the Seine a bit."

George stood up from the table, smiled and said, "Right. That's that sorted then. We'll wait for you in the lounge on Thursday morning Jo. Until then, you both have a lovely day tomorrow, we're off to bed" George helped Edith to her feet.

"Good night luvvies," Edith said and they left the bar.

"He's a dirty old man; did you see the twinkle he had in his eye when he said they were off to bed?" Jo asked as she watched them leave the room. "They're going to be good fun; I'm looking forward to being with them. Are you sure you don't want to come along Zara?"

"I'm sure; it's not really my sort of thing, to be honest with you, Jo. You go and don't worry about me, you didn't this morning when you left me alone with a strange man," Zara said with a wink and they both laughed.

"Right let's have a night cap, look at the map and plan our trip to Napoleon's tomb then, shall we?" Zara took the map out of her handbag and spread it out on the table.

CHAPTER NINE

The following morning, Zara and Jo, as planned, travelled via the metro to visit 'Hotel des Invalides' to see Napoleon's Tomb.

"You have to put a euro in the slot and choose the language you want," Zara translated the written notice for Jo and watched her put the euro in, press the button for English and place the headphones over her ears. Giving Zara the thumbs up sign she walked along the marble passageway and around the outside of the central tomb.

Zara watched her stop at each small alcove to view the small tombs that held Napoleon's brothers and some of his loyal men. The look of concentration on Jo's face made Zara smile; she had never seen Jo look so serious and had not realised, until now, how important this visit to Napoleon's tomb was for Jo.

Jo had asked Zara to translate everything she could and insisted on knowing all that was printed about Napoleon in the tour guide. Now she was listening to an oral guide to the tomb itself. Zara followed Jo as she walked down the marble steps leading to Napoleon's tomb; she could understand the amazement that Jo must have felt as a youngster viewing the great tomb. It was so elaborate with its gold decoration and laurel leaved carvings in the different types of wood. The written signs stated that the woods were of mahogany, ebony and oak. Zara gazed up at the frescos on the domed ceiling above her. 'This is stunning,' Zara thought. 'So much detail and hard work must have been put into this.' Zara's thoughts were interrupted by Jo.

"It says that he *is* inside, but he's entombed in a nest of six coffins all made from different materials," Jo told Zara as she quite quickly walked around the grand tomb.

"Right that's that then. Come on," Jo pulled off the headphones, placed them back on the shelf and started to walk back up the stairs.

"Where are you going Jo?" Zara asked, slightly worried by Jo's haste.

"He's definitely in there. It said so. That's it then," Jo replied brusquely as she marched up the marble steps, stopping at the top, waiting for Zara to join her.

"What do you mean, 'that's it then'?" Zara shouted up at Jo who was leaning over the marble balustrade looking down at her.

"I mean, I know now. I know he's in there; I can feel it. All of these years I've been wanting to return to see/feel it myself; it's all very well reading it on Wikipedia that he's in there but I couldn't really be sure until I saw and felt it for myself. Me and

'Na-Bo' have a rapport you know?," Jo said with a smile on her face.

Zara was confused. Jo had made such a fuss about 'needing' to see the tomb and now she was here, she had hardly looked at it. She hadn't noticed the ornamentation, the gold, the carvings, nor had she looked upwards to the beautiful frescos. "*That's it then*," Zara mimicked Jo's voice as she started to climb the steps. She turned around and looked back at the tomb, "*He's In there then,*" she said softly to herself, laughing at this escapade.

When she joined Jo at the top, she received a great hug and a kiss on the lips, "What was that for?" she asked Jo.

"Just a thanks for being a great mate and coming here with me. I know you think I'm a bit daft, but I had to find out for myself and I know now…"

Zara broke into Jo's sentence and they finished it together, "He really is in there." They laughed together and linked arms as they strolled out into the sunshine. Zara really loved Jo and was sure she would always hold this trip to Paris precious in her memory.

Arm in arm, Zara and Jo strolled down the 'Esplanade des Invalides' making their way to the bridge that crosses the Seine to the Champs-Elysees. They talked about the people they had met so far and the experiences they had shared together;

likening it to their misadventures and experiences in their youth when they were growing up together.

Zara was so glad she had reunited with Jo; her painstaking career goals had pulled them apart. She made herself a vow that she would not let this happen again when they returned to England, and to work. As close as she felt to Jo, she still had not revealed her dance experience on the ferry. Somehow she felt that if she did 'tell', it would make the memory fade a little. And besides, she quite liked having a secret.

"I feel like a new woman Jo, a 're-born' Zara. This Paris air must be having an effect on me, too."

"It's not the air Zara; it's the freedom of no routine, no work and not having to live your life through your career."

"I feel different now; I no longer feel like just a career woman, a wall flower; I feel I am an English rose," Zara said echoing the artist's words, whilst posing like a model on the bridge's parapet.

"A Venus fly trap's more likely," Jo muttered leaning over the parapet to look at the waters below. There was an empty barge heading for the arch under Zara and Jo. They watched as the bargee shouted to two children playing a game on the roof of the barge.

Zara's mind wandered back to the ferry and the feel of the Armani jacket around her shoulders, warming her on that chilly night and placed there by her gallant friend Noel. He had obviously made an impact on her as she was still thinking about him and not work. 'But was this good?' she asked herself. It seemed to her that she had jumped out of the frying pan and into the fire; yet again one thing was governing her thoughts. She must forget him; she probably would never see him again anyway. She must think of him only as a beautiful fantasy, saved for moments of private sensual pleasures. Zara giggled as she formed the thought.

"That was a dirty giggle. What are you thinking of?" Jo asked nudging Zara's arm for a reply.

"I'm thinking that we have not seen the famous 'red light' district yet. Let's spend our last evening there. What do you think?" Zara replied, thinking quickly, to avoid disclosing her secret.

Jo smiled, linked Zara's arm with her own and steered her to cross the bridge, "I think that that is a fantastic idea and I still want to see you in my black lace dress; that will be the perfect place to wear it. Come on, let's grab some of that free food at the hotel and 'play' with makeup and clothes for the rest of the afternoon; like we used to when we were teenagers and our only worry was, 'Take That' may split up."

The taxi picked them up at the hotel. The taxi driver was used to tourists and filled them in on 'Quartier Pigalle', the place where the theatres, clubs, sex shops and adult shows were gathered together in Paris. He informed them that the allied soldiers, during world war two, nicknamed the area of Pigalle, 'Pig Alley'.

He dropped them off at the top of a long street. There seemed to be people everywhere; some were strolling along viewing the merchandise while others were chatting in doorways, in their cars and some were stopped in the road. Music streamed out of the club doors as anyone exited or entered; the aroma of wine, beer and good times wafted onto the street; and the street lights and neon signs illuminated the pedestrians, lighting up the highlights in the women's hair and casting shadows on the sensuous mouths that were stating the prices.

Jo stood on the pavement waiting for Zara to pay the driver. Jo re-adjusted the short black leather skirt she was wearing as the tops of her stockings were showing. Her cream cropped blouse accentuated her narrow waist much to her satisfaction.

It had been Jo that had chosen their clothes for the evening and she had chosen the black lace dress for Zara. It had been the right choice as Zara looked terrific; the dress clung to her body like a second skin and left very little to the imagination.

"Right then, let's stroll down 'Pig Alley' and see what's on offer," Jo said taking Zara's arm in her own.

They passed several bars and a couple of strip tease shows when Zara pointed to a poster on a large pillar outside an ornate building. The poster showed the bodies of a black man and a white woman interlinked in an embrace of sorts.

"This looks a little different Jo. What do you think, shall we try it?" Zara asked.

"I've never had the pleasure of a glorious ebony skin; let's find out if what they say is true," Jo nudged Zara's arm and winked.

They turned into the pillared entrance and walked through a gilded hallway to a large double doorway at the end. Here they were greeted by a smiling receptionist who took their money and introduced them whilst handing them over to a large, black man dressed in a tuxedo who opened the door and led them inside by taking each of them by their arms.

"I am Lewis and I will escort you to your seats and, if you will allow me, I will be your protector for the evening's entertainment," he said in his deep sexy baritone voice.

Zara and Jo looked up at their escort's smiling face and then looked at each other. Jo winked at Zara and replied, "Thank you. That would suit us nicely."

Lewis led them to a long velveteen seat in a dark corner of the room and whilst he was discussing what drinks he would recommend with Jo, Zara looked around the room.

Each of the seating compartments was separated by thin railings running from the ceiling to the floor, lit only by small lights around the table tops. The central stage area and the walls around the seating area were draped with velvet curtains, giving the feel of intimacy with the stage; Zara wondered what was behind the stage curtains.

The show had not yet started and people were still taking their seats. A waitress, dressed in a black PVC cat suit, brought their drinks to the table. Zara watched as Lewis ran his hands over the waitress's backside as she bent to place the drinks on the table.

"Flo is one of our many beautiful dancing cats," he said as Flo walked away with a wiggle.

Jo clinked glasses with Zara and nodded her appreciation in Lewis's direction and gave Zara that 'meaningful' wink again.

Zara could feel the excitement building up in her stomach; this night club was so different; she felt out of her comfort zone but stimulated by the fear; she also felt a thrill of the unknown that in turn ignited a sexual arousal deep inside her.

A roll of drums interrupted Zara's thoughts and she turned to look at a spotlight that had appeared in front of the curtains on the stage. Suspended in the spotlight was a cage made of strong leather, large enough to hold a standing person comfortably. Through the leather bars, Zara could see a young girl in her early twenties. Her muscular body was glistening from the light's reflection; she was wearing a thin leather thong that started from around her neck and crisscrossed her torso and followed on down between her thighs. She had flat leather sandals on her feet with leather thongs entwined up her calves, ending at the top of her thighs; her wrists were also wrapped in thongs, but they were tied behind her back making her breasts jut forward. She stood still and quiet in her leather cage but Zara could see the flash of anger in her eyes and the tight lipped 'no surrender' look on her face.

Lewis leant forward and told them both, "Enjoy. Do not worry, she may be small but she is tough and as strong as an ox. She will enjoy."

Zara looked back at the stage and saw that the cage was now rotating slowly so that the audience could have an all round view of the captive.

The drums started up a rhythmic beat and the girl's body moved in a syncopated rhythm alongside of the drums. The tempo sped up, the cage then started to move with the girl. Zara noticed that the girl's face had changed; her eyes were no longer flashing their anger, now they held eroticism and her tongue was travelling over her lips making them glisten with moist expectance.

Crack... Crack... Zara looked to where the new sound was coming from and noticed the large whips at either side of the cage held by two blonde women, twins, who had now stepped into the spotlight. These women were dressed in tight black leather trousers and black stilettos. They wore nothing to cover their beautiful pale skinned breasts but both had a thick gold band around their necks and their fingers were covered with rings that caught the light when their wrists cracked the whips. They both had silver blonde hair tied up in tight buns on the top of their heads.

Zara now remembered Lewis's words, "I shall be your protector for the evening." The feeling of erotic fear returned to her stomach. She watched the two women as they drew nearer to the girl in the cage, their whips ever closer to the bare skin inside. At every crack, Zara felt herself wince but the young girl did not seem in the least frightened; in fact she looked like she was on the point of orgasm. Her body was writhing to the music and the thongs between her thighs were glistening with the signs of her moist pleasure.

The cage was slowly being lowered to the floor and the two women were now standing very close to it, legs apart in a dominant pose, staring out at their audience. As the cage hit the floor, the curtains behind them dropped, revealing a wide stage. The stage floor had a pathway of men lying head to toe in a row, stomach and heads down to face the floor; one black skinned one white skinned, one black, one white and so on; their bare backsides giving the appearance of a row of hills on the horizon. At the top of the pathway was a large, ornate wooden chair, carved with gold tribal markings. Seated on it was a beautiful golden skinned woman with long plaited strawberry blonde hair that was entwined with gold braid giving the illusion that her hair was aflame; she was a golden Amazon.

The Amazon stood up displaying her height of about six feet. All she was wearing was a thin rectangular piece of golden silk that covered her neck to her toes, which were free of any footwear. The material had small, gold chains attached to the sides exposing the woman's hips and her legs when she walked. She walked regally forwards, onto and over the male bodies that made up her pathway to the cage. Each of her footsteps were placed on the black and white skinned cheeks of the men beneath her. Zara could see her toes curling around the soft, firm flesh that she trod upon, making each footstep into an erotic movement.

Inside the cage, the girl was now still, watching. The twins on either side had pushed their whip handles through the leather bars and were holding her legs apart, trapped between the bars and the whip handles; the girl could not move her legs. The queen arrived at the cage and the drum beat ceased; there was silence.

Zara was startled out of her trancelike stare by the absence of the drums. She turned to look at Jo, who was also watching the stage enthralled by the action. Zara noticed a glint of something metallic

DESTINY

under the table and realised it was Lewis's watch; she could not see his hand but she knew by the change in Jo's face where the hand was heading and therefore, turned her face quickly back to the stage.

The Amazonian Queen's arms were now reaching up to the top of the cage and were untying the cord that held the leather bars in place. The twins removed their whips and the bars fell, in a spider pattern around the cage onto the floor. The girl stood defiant whilst the twins ran the tips of their whips over her shoulders and down again to her thighs, which had remained wide apart throughout, and trapped them only this time between themselves and their whips. The girl remained captive. Judging by the look on the girl's face Zara thought, escape was the last thing on her mind.

The queen placed one finger on the nape of the girl's neck and ran it slowly down her spine until it reached the top of the cleft in her backside. She pushed the girl's back so that her body doubled over, exposing her buttocks. The Queen then ran her fingers over the muscular girl's buttocks, taking her time when she touched the moist thong closest to the girl's thighs. With one quick sharp movement, she slapped her hand across the girl's bottom making the girl shudder; Zara was not sure whether the shudder was in response to shock or pleasure.

The Queen then walked around to the girl's front and lifted her face up with the palm of her hand. The girl stared defiantly at the Queen. The Queen smiled pursing her lips to blow a kiss to the

93

girl. With the palm of her hand, she raised the girl's head, so that she was back to a standing position and proceeded to caress the front of the girl's body with her fingertips. The girl and the Queen maintained eye contact throughout the caress, with the girl's eyes showing the pleasure she was receiving. The Queen removed her fingertips from the girl, leaving her lust showing openly to the audience in the form of swollen breasts and erect nipples.

The Queen stood back from the girl and made a hand gesture to the twins. It was now their turn. In unison they rolled their whip handles up the girl's inner thighs and the audience was given the full view of the un-caged girl's wet readiness. One twin angled her whip so that its blunt end was just touching the outer lips of the girl's labia; the other twin took the thong end of the whip and traced a path down the girl's body leaving the tip of the thong dangling over the clitoral tip that was now poking out from beneath its sheath. The girl pushed her hips forward to gain a firmer touch from her tormenters but received a slap across the face from the Queen and a full kiss on the lips directly afterwards.

The Queen then turned abruptly from the girl and proceeded to walk into the audience. She walked directly to a table close to where Zara and Jo were, where a man was sitting alone. She took him by the hand and led him onto the stage and into the spotlight. She took both of his hands and placed them on the girl's breasts, where they hung free in his cupped palms. The man needed no guidance as to what to do next.

Zara watched his thumbs trace circles around the girl's nipples, making her own stand erect in response, as though feeling what the girl was feeling.

The Queen made some sort of signal and the drums returned with the tribal rhythm of before and the pathway of men moved from their positions on the floor and encircled the man and the girl with a tribal dance.

Zara could not see the two in the middle any longer as the dance grew faster and faster and the stage was taken over with dancing bodies. The men were wearing leather pouches with thonged backs which showed every movement of their firm buttocks. Zara was again left in a trance as she watched their muscular bodies move to the earthy beat that held a similarity to the reggae that she loved.

Suddenly behind her the curtain drapes that enclosed the audience and stage, were released revealing more beautiful male and female bodies dancing erotically around her.

The couple directly behind her was dancing in on and around the bars that separated the seats, stroking each other's bodies when they came close enough to touch. Zara recognised one of the dancers, Flo the waitress that had brought their drinks earlier. She watched as Jo and Lewis stood up and joined the dancers with their own intimate dancing. Zara smiled at Jo and then turned her gaze back to the stage.

The Queen's twin assistants were unfastening the gold chains that held the silk material that the Queen was wearing. The twins removed the silk that covered the Queen's body and then the music stopped, as did the dancers. Slowly the dancers in the circle returned to their face down positions on the floor. Zara could now see the man from the audience, and the captive girl in the centre. The man had been stripped of his shirt and was standing, bare chested, held by the arms of the strong girl behind him. The captive was now the one in command; the man was facing the audience and Zara could see his face. She leant forward to get a better look and then turned to Jo for a second opinion, but Jo was gone and Lewis with her. Zara looked back again to the stage and received assurance that her eyes were not playing tricks; it was Noel. Her infatuation from the ferry. He was standing half naked being held by his temptress in a submissive posture.

The Queen, now naked but for her gold neck band, walked slowly towards Noel, with her impressive Amazonian body having an obvious effect upon him. One twin handed some material to the Queen which she proceeded to tie around Noel's eyes. Noel now stood captive and blindfolded.

Zara's thoughts turned to fantasies. He was there just ready for the taking with his body yielding to these women, but not to her. She wanted him so badly for only herself. She stood up to gain a clearer view of the stage. The Queen caught Zara's movement and beckoned her to come closer. Zara walked across the stage and stood in front of Noel.

This was her fantasy becoming reality; he was now hers to do with as she wished. She moved her mouth to his neck and traced a pattern with her tongue across his Adam's apple and up behind one ear, where she nipped his skin with her teeth causing him to exhale deeply. Her fingers played with the blonde curls on his chest and moved to the top of his trousers where they ran their tips just inside the waistband. Noel inhaled to give Zara more access to the bulge that had grown in his trousers; her tongue followed her fingers and toyed with the hollow of his belly button. Zara felt the Queen's breasts brush against her back as she leant down to whisper in her ear, "Carry on. He's all yours, my sweet."

Zara took Noel's hands and placed them on her breasts, rotating the palms across her nipples which were hard under her lace. Someone in the audience whistled loudly shaking Zara out of her reverie. What was she doing? She had forgotten about the audience. Zara stood back, embarrassed. The Queen smiled and called forward one of her male slaves to escort Zara back to her seat. The slave scooped Zara up in his large oiled arms and carried her back to her seat, to the sound of whistles and applause from the audience. Then the show continued.

Zara felt awkward and embarrassed but the audience was once again enthralled by the show and concentrating their attention upon the stage. Zara found her drink, to give her something to do with her hands and sat down in the dark cubicle again. Jo and Lewis were still absent and nowhere to be seen. 'So much for my protector for the evening,' Zara thought. But her mind was in turmoil; she felt the urge to run back to the hotel, leaving Jo here alone. She could not stay here by herself, but she couldn't just leave without trying to find her friend. Her decision made, Zara stood and with one last look towards the stage to see Noel now in the beautiful Queen's hands, she left to enquire at the reception of Jo's whereabouts.

CHAPTER TEN

Zara woke late and missed the hotel's breakfast. She noticed there was a note stuck to the mirror on the dressing table at the end of the bed.

Popped back and didn't want to wake you. Have caught the coach to Disneyland; will catch up on the news when I get back. Have a lovely day, see you tonight.

Love Jo xx

Zara was glad that she was alone. She did not want to speak to Jo until she had managed to sort things out in her own head. What a night. Did it really happen? It was Noel, she was certain of that; she could recognise his scent anywhere. She smiled to herself; she was the stranger this time. He could not possibly have known that it had been her that had touched him. She had one regret though; she wished that there had not been an audience. Yes, she was a more daring woman since taking this holiday but she still did not want to share such an intimate moment with a room full of strangers. This would probably never change; especially at the thought of sharing a man that instilled such lust inside of her. She ought to feel pleased with her further encounter with him, but she did not. There was just something about him, something that she found irresistible. And she just found herself desiring him even more.

Zara pulled herself up and out of the bed and went into the bathroom to turn the shower on. She needed a cold shower this morning. That would wake her up. In the bathroom Zara looked into the mirror; there written in lipstick was another message from Jo:

Had my ebony man and it is all true…

Zara laughed. She had not seen Jo since last night at the club, when she had found the receptionist who told her that Jo had left a message for her, telling her not to worry as she would not be back at the hotel and to get a taxi back without her. Zara left the club and had caught a taxi alone.

After her shower, Zara pottered around the room collecting her few belongings together, readying to pack that evening. She found Jo's clothes from the night before in a pile on the floor, dropped where they had been taken off. She opened the wardrobe door and took out what her mother would have called a 'summer frock'. It was feminine and flowery, just the sort of dress that went with her old image. She would wear it one last time and leave it, along with the old Zara, in the hotel waste bin when they left Paris. She brushed her long black hair and tied it up into a ribbon, then turned and viewed herself in the mirror. This was the old Zara, smart and respectable. But now, under her clothes, she felt different. She was more confident in her sexuality. She decided that she would take a leisurely walk to visit 'Notre Dame' and say goodbye to the old Zara along the way.

Outside the sun shone and the air smelled beautiful. As Zara took in big lungfuls of the air, she remembered that she had not had any breakfast. The fresh air and walk had made her hungry. She passed a small take-away snack bar and grabbed herself a baguette filled with salad and brie. She strolled along the side of the River Seine munching her late breakfast and enjoying the tranquillity after the storm of the last few days.

Her thoughts returned to England and work. She thought about Shelia: she would have loads to tell her when she returned. Shelia was unshockable, but would she take to Zara's new image? It would not affect her work of course, Zara was forever the professional, but it could actually have a positive effect on their male clients. Sheila would at least appreciate that, Zara was thinking when she looked up and saw 'Notre Dame' on the other side of the river from her current position, with its dominant structure overpowering the old city around it. It looked quite dark and threatening from a distance and Zara stood for a while gazing at its gothic splendour. She could imagine it in the evening when the up lighting would cast eerie shadows on the grounds around it. She could see the tourists flocking around it. There were crowds of them, people of all ages and cultures coming to view a piece of history, take a few snaps and leave it all behind a little more worn by the thousands of footsteps that had trod in and around it.

Zara walked across the bridge that connected the small island to the large city, and over the large paved area that led to the entrance. Inside it felt cold and was dark as the only light was the sunlight pouring through the huge circular rose window in the south wall. Zara looked at the rainbow of colours that were patterned onto the floor from the stained glass of the window; it was stunning. She read in the placard that it was a gift from King Saint Louis. 'What a gift; she thought as thousands of people had been able to appreciate it. She strolled around the building viewing the sculptures and the carvings; learning about the ten years it had taken to clean the building. Zara thought she heard a bat flying high up in the ceiling and she was reminded of the story of the hunchback. 'Poor unloved man,' she thought. She shivered, partly from the chill in the building and partly for the memory of the hunchback. It was cold in here after the heat outside, so she made her way to the door and the warmth of the sunshine. She found a seat outside under the huge towers and looked up at the gargoyles carved into the stone. The seat was warm and she loved the feel of the sun shining down upon her; she closed her eyes and listened to the tourists mingling around the building and the babble of different languages. An English voice near to her made her open her eyes.

"Of course it is only a story but people like the romance of these old buildings don't they?"

'That sounds familiar,' Zara thought. She was sure she recognised the polite, gentlemanly voice and instantly an image of blue eyes shot into her mind. It was Noel's voice, she was certain. She turned her head to see him relating the story of *The Hunchback of Notre Dame*, to a smartly dressed man of about the same age standing with him. Zara could not believe her luck. She felt this time she must act or perhaps she may never see him again. To have been so lucky this far to see him twice in such a large city; she was sure it wouldn't happen again. She stood up and moved nearer to them.

"Hello Noel, isn't it? Remember me, we had a chat on the ferry," Zara said holding her hand out in greeting to him. Noel's face turned to face hers and she thought she caught a slight blush to his cheeks, when he took her hand and held it for a short while.

"Hello Zara. Fancy meeting you here. Are you enjoying your holiday?"

"Yes, thank you. I have had a wonderful time," she could not resist adding, "I hope it hasn't been all business for you here this time."

The gentleman that was with Noel nudged his arm and said, "Well are you going to keep this lovely lady to yourself or do I get an introduction?"

Noel apologised to his friend and introduced him, "This is Philippe, a business associate of mine. Philippe this is Zara."

Zara took his hand and enjoyed a warm, handshake with him.

"Nice to meet you. You are on holiday. When do you return to England?" he asked smiling warmly at Zara.

"Tomorrow morning. Today is my last day in Paris." Zara returned his warm smile.

Philippe looked at Noel, and suggested, "You must come and have lunch with us then. We have a table booked at a restaurant nearby. I am sure they can squeeze a beautiful woman in. What do you think Noel?"

Noel looked straight into Zara's eyes, making her stomach flip nervously. "That would be lovely. What do you say Zara, will you join us?"

Zara smiled returning Noel's gaze and said, "Thank you I would love to join you."

Philippe took Zara's arm and steered her towards the bridge leaving Noel to follow them.

"So you met Noel on the ferry over, I hope his company was pleasant and he didn't bore you with his business deals. He can be quite insufferable sometimes," Philippe said in a joking manner.

Zara looked at Noel, who was now walking on the other side of Philippe.

"We had an interesting conversation and I wasn't the slightest bit bored. Do you work with

Noel in England or are you one of his 'business deals'?" Zara asked.

"I live in Paris and am Noel's Parisian connection; we go to the shows together and I introduce him to all the beautiful models and their designers. I'm his contact for the parties, where he makes his connections, aren't I Noel?"

Noel nodded but did not look very amused at his friend's comments.

Zara felt very relaxed and comfortable in the knowledge that she knew something that Noel did not and liked this advantage.

"You obviously socialise together on your evenings off. Did you go anywhere nice last night?" Zara had to ask, she wanted to know how Noel would reply.

"I went to one of our designers' birthday parties at his chateau on the outskirts of Paris but Noel was tied up in a meeting and couldn't make it. Shame as he missed a great evening's entertainment," Philippe answered.

Zara smiled, "What a shame you got 'tied up' Noel; I hope you weren't held captive all night?" Zara looked straight into Noel's eyes, her own laughing with their secret knowledge.

Noel was obvious feeling uncomfortable about it all as he made a large gesture to point out that they had arrived at the restaurant; this stopped the conversation as they went inside and were shown to their table, now for three.

Zara only had a small amount to eat but enjoyed herself tremendously. Every opportunity that allowed her to comment on the previous night's antics, she took making subtle innuendos. Noel did not comment but Zara caught him frowning a couple of times. Philippe flirted with her throughout the meal and she not only let him, she positively encouraged him. Philippe asked Zara what she did for a living and she told him about the Personnel agency and Sheila. He seemed overly interested, which made Zara feel flattered by his attention but there was something about him that made her feel odd. She didn't know why, and she could not quite put her finger on it, so she just went with the flow and enjoyed his company.

By the time coffee was served, Zara noticed that Noel was not happy; was he jealous? She wondered.

"You are not with your friend Zara. Has she deserted you?" Noel enquired sharply.

"She went to Disneyland with the coach passengers today. I preferred to spend my last day in the relative quiet of the older part of the city," Zara replied calmly worried that the buoyant new Zara had ruffled Noel's feathers.

"Well we'd better leave you in peace then. We wouldn't want to disturb your tranquil time," Noel said as he stood up and went to pay the bill.

"He is not in a pleasant mood. I will apologise for him," Philippe said trying to smooth the atmosphere that had built up. "Zara, before we leave may I have your business card? We are often in need of temporary personnel here and I am sure your company provides the most efficient people. You do cater to the mainland, don't you?"

"Yes of course we do Philippe, many of our personnel speak 3 languages; some even speak 4. It would be a pleasure to work with you, I am sure," Zara said rummaging in her bag and handing him her card. "Just contact my number and you will get through to me personally." She then stood up, shook Philippe by the hand and thanked him for lunch.

Noel appeared by her side holding her jacket for her to put on.

"The gentleman as always; thank you Noel for the lunch, and the company." Zara offered her hand to him. Noel ignored it and leant to kiss her on the cheek, as he did so he whispered into her ear "You wicked woman. It was you last night, touché," he looked at her and said out loud. "Til we meet again, mon cherie. Au revoir," and he turned and walked away with Philippe.

The incident reminded Zara of their abrupt goodbye on the ferry but this time the boot was on the other foot. It was Noel who was now embarrassed and wanted to vacate immediately. When had he twigged? She wondered and thought it must have been early during lunch as that was when his mood had changed.

She left the restaurant and watched the two men walk away down the street. What had she done? She was so stupid. She had enjoyed the power that she had had over Noel during lunch, more than his actual company, and she let him slip away from her yet again. When would she learn? Her meetings with Noel seemed to be more a battle of wills than a meeting of two friends. Zara shrugged and walked in the opposite direction to return to her last day in Paris; now though, it didn't seem so tranquil.

CHAPTER ELEVEN

The coach journey to Calais consisted of each person suggesting a song to sing. Everybody joined in, even the spotty teenagers; it was full of camaraderie; people who had not had much to say during the holiday were bursting with it now. Edith and Jo entertained everybody with a duet of, 'We'll Meet Again' which brought an odd tear to the eyes of the sentimental and tears of laughter from the rest, as the pair were wearing Donald Duck baseball caps and Mickey Mouse t-shirts.

Zara felt a little sad that their holiday was now over, but Jo cheered her up by enlightening her with the lustful details of her 'ebony protector'. Zara said nothing of her encounters with Noel, though. Jo didn't ask so Zara felt that it should be left unsaid. She had never been one for 'kissing and telling'; this made her secret more precious to her. They separated on the ferry as Jo was asked to play backgammon with her friends, George and Edith. Zara wasn't in the mood for company and took herself outside to watch the ocean and to think.

It was warm on the deck. It did not seem quite so romantic in the daylight though. Zara watched the seagulls flying alongside of the ferry. They seemed to be attached by a piece of fine string, keeping in perfect line with the ferry's movements and screeching out their woeful cries for alms. She wondered where they nested, as they always seemed to be following the ferries to and fro from port to port. One bird flew very close to her and she caught his beady eye with her own; he reminded her of a man out on the prowl. Men, seagulls… they're all the same, just out for what they can get, she thought. But then she cringed, who was she to talk? She'd just been acting in a similar manner on this holiday. She smirked. Yes she had, but hadn't it been fun? she thought. Girl power: she could go for that.

The holiday was now taking its toll. Most people slept on the return journey to Leicester. At the coach station there were tearful goodbyes from some and the taking of telephone numbers and exchanges of addresses from others. Jo said goodbye to George and Edith and promised to visit them soon.

"Will you really?" Zara asked her on their way home.

"Yes, I think I will. I really enjoyed their company yesterday. They are a really good laugh and fun to be with. I want to be like them when I'm their age," Jo said in reminiscence.

The taxi pulled up outside Zara's flat.

"Bye for now. I'll phone you in the week. Don't work too hard and remember the new image," were Jo's parting words to Zara.

Zara dumped her suitcase in the hall and went to put the kettle on, picking up her mail to read on the way to the kitchen. Bills, bills and more bills. No nice letters, just bills and junk mail, the latter of which she threw in the bin. The answering machine was not much better. A message from her Mum asking her to call her when she got home and a message from her gym, telling her they were running a sponsored spinning class and would be grateful if she could collect sponsors for the event. 'Obviously nobody's missed me,' Zara thought as she sat at the kitchen table sipping her tea.

Exhausted, she turned off the lights, picked up her bag and went upstairs for a longed-for soak in the bath. Tomorrow she would phone Mother and catch up on any family gossip. She would probably be invited to have Sunday lunch, if she played her cards right; there was nothing in her fridge and she could do with some good old English home cooking.

It felt a bit of a letdown to be home after all the week's antics. 'Sort of lonely, she thought. She was already missing Jo's dirty laughter and jokes. She thought maybe she should phone her to arrange an evening in where she could repay her for the amazing holiday. And then Zara's mind returned to that first afternoon in the hotel room and she thought, 'Mmmm that's a good idea,' Zara smiled to herself.

The phone had not stopped at work all the next Monday morning so Zara didn't even get a chance to tell Shelia about her excursion until late in the afternoon. They chatted for the best part of an hour. Shelia made her first comment on Zara's new image; she said Zara looked different somehow.

"That's because I feel different Shelia. I'm more complete and I feel I could take on the world right now," Zara told Shelia.

"Just our clients will do," Shelia said. "And there are plenty of those at the moment. We will have to advertise for more temps at this rate."

Business was definitely taking an up-turn and Zara was glad that she had taken the holiday whilst she had been able to. There would be no chance of another for a while.

"About this painting. How exactly were you posing?" Sheila enquired tactfully.

"Oh that. Well we didn't pose exactly; we were sleeping whilst he painted," Zara replied flippantly.

"I see," said Shelia not really understanding how a person asleep could be of interest to an art collector.

"The artist promised that he would send a photograph of it. He has my address; I promise to show it to you, when it arrives," Zara said to deter any further investigation from Shelia.

Zara was sitting at her desk, looking at a list of the new personnel that Shelia had taken on whilst she had been away. "I see that you have sent a male secretary to T and M merchandise. Is that wise? You know how old fashioned they are."

"Wise? You have yet to meet him; he certainly knows his job. He will be a great asset to the company. I am sure he will get the new Zara's approval," Shelia said with a twinkle in her eye.

"I see. Taking on young intelligent men for your employ now, are you? It will take more than a pretty face to impress me. You're showing a weakness in your old age Shelia," Zara said teasingly, "Well that's me finished for the day. I will work through all the paperwork during the week while you are off gallivanting around the country."

"I will not be gallivanting. I will be obtaining new customers and charming old ones. Those are the perks of being the boss," Shelia retorted as they walked out of the office together. "Anyway, you have had your fair share of gallivanting, young miss."

"I suppose so. It's back to the grindstone now," Zara said with an exaggerated grimace, making Shelia laugh.

The week seemed to drag on for Zara. There was so much paper work to go through and be logged onto the computer's filing system, this being the tedious part of her work that had to be done in order to make her job easier when locating personnel once completed.

Zara telephoned Jo in the middle of the week and they arranged to meet up on the Saturday night and have a few drinks at their local pub. She was looking forward to seeing Jo again; she had missed her friend's company this week.

Saturday duly arrived. Zara shopped during the day for new shoes, handbag, skirt, dress, jacket and lingerie; all were needed to keep up her new image. After all the hard earned money of the past few months, it was time to now spend, and spend she did.

On return, full of excitement with her purchases, Zara almost missed the letter on her doormat. Glancing down her heart skipped a beat when she noticed the French postmark. Her fingers trembled as she felt the outline of a photograph, the photograph; the missing piece of the holiday jigsaw. She opened the envelope and removed its contents. The photograph fell to the floor and landed face up exposing the intimacy that she and Jo had enjoyed that night.

Zara felt the familiar stirrings in her body return. It was more than just Jo's company that she had missed, it was her touch also. Those expert fingers and that darting tongue were expert in sending quivers of pleasure through to her erogenous zones.

Zara wondered whether Jo felt the same way about her in different circumstances.

The letter was still in Zara's hand waiting to be read. Her eyes would not leave the photograph though. She wanted to read the letter but was captivated by the image on the doormat. Memories of those missing hours started slowly to return. She could feel Jo's lips pressing on her abdomen. She could remember the simultaneous orgasms that had occurred. She heard her own voice cry out as Jo's fingertips caressed her clitoris and the sensation of her own fingers sliding within Jo's moisture. The giving and receiving of the most precious pleasure that can be shared between two women was there on the floor at her feet.

Zara tore herself away from the memories to read the letter:

My beautiful English roses

Thank you. I have enough to eat for many months. Please find the promised photograph enclosed. I hope it pleases. If you return to Paris, please spend some time with me. We make nature together.

Yours naturally, Didiet

Didiet, so that was his name. Zara laughed to herself, her artist lover was no longer anonymous. "Didiet," she spoke his name out loud; she liked the feel of the vowels on her tongue. Didiet, Didiet, she repeated the name over again until she was singing it as she ran up the stairs to run the bath. The photograph remained, lying in all its splendour on the doormat of Zara's front door.

The pub was half full by the time Zara arrived. In one corner a television was blaring out and the commentator was stating that the score was one nil with only nine minutes left of the game. Several men were gathered around it making what Zara thought were Neanderthal noises directed at the screen. Zara looked around and located Jo sitting at a table in the far corner from the television.

"You look terrific, Zara. Is that new clobber you're wearing?" Jo asked, admiring Zara's outfit.

"Went shopping, and this isn't all I bought. I spent a few hundred today. I thought I deserved to treat myself with all that overtime I earned this last year. I'm glad you like it, this was chosen specifically for you," Zara said, making eye contact with Jo, knowing that it was unlikely that the suggestion in Zara's voice would be missed by her close friend.

"Amber really makes your hair sparkle. I've never seen velvet in that colour before," Jo reached out to touch the shoulder strap of Zara's skimpy dress; she ran her fingers over the smooth material, making sure to skim Zara's skin whilst doing so.

Zara felt the tips of Jo's fingers touch her and knew that her friend's feelings had not changed, even if the circumstances had. "I received a letter today, from a man called Didiet," Zara said in a matter of fact voice. "A letter that's contents might be of some interest to you." Zara's eyes twinkled in the fun.

Jo took a sip of her drink and muttered very quietly to Zara, "Have you seen who's heading this way?"

Zara turned to look and saw three men walking towards their table. One of them was her ex, an old boyfriend from her school days, Mark. He was the boy (now man) she had lost her virginity to and was her first relationship even, it could be said, her first love. She turned back to face Jo and coolly continued with her conversation. "In fact I *know* the contents of this letter will interest you. Would it help if I told you the envelope had a French stamp on it?"

"Zara! Didn't you hear me? It's Mark and some of his cronies and they're heading this way. Aren't you the slightest bit interested?"

The three men arrived at the table, two of them pulling up extra chairs to seat themselves. Mark had already taken the only available seat, the one next to Zara.

"Hi Zara, I haven't seen you around for a while." Zara remembered Mark's vain macho voice; he was so cock sure of himself that she felt irritated by his presence. The last time she had seen him was when she left school to go on to university several years ago, at her parents' insistence. They had encouraged her to spread her wings as they knew she had the intelligence to take her chosen career to its limits. Zara at the time had been full of self-doubt and Mark was totally against her leaving. Looking back on it though, she realised that a lot of her self-doubt had appeared when she was with Mark. He had always been putting her down and putting her in her place, the place, at least, he wanted her to be in – his possession. Seeing him again now made her wonder whether he was part of the reason she had lacked confidence in her sexuality.

"Hello Mark. You haven't seen me because I've been working and out of the country for a while," Zara said wanting him to know that she was managing very well without him, "Jo and I spent a week in Paris recently, as a matter of fact. Living it up and deservedly so, after months of hard work." Zara could not believe her calm assertive voice. She had no interest in this man; in fact he was getting in the way of her plans for the evening. She finished the remains of her drink and made a move to stand up.

Jo, picking up on Zara's vibes, grabbed her coat and stood up also leaving the remainder of her drink on the table.

"Excuse us. We have a date elsewhere. We haven't got time to chat. Bye everyone," Zara tried to leave but Mark sat up blocking her exit. "Very funny Mark, move your legs please," Zara said not in the least amused by his antics.

"Don't go Zara, I need to talk to you," he said putting an arm out to stop her. "You look beautiful, and sexy in that dress." Mark's hand started to wander over Zara's velvet covered backside.

Zara pushed his hand away, "This is not yours," Zara said indicating her body. "I am not owned by you or anyone else. Now move before I shout to the Landlord." Zara eyes flashed in anger, and saw him turn from a cocky young man into a small hurt boy. She remembered he would have this reaction each time they argued and he didn't get his own way; back then her heart would melt and he'd suck her back in to being his possession. But not anymore.

Jo spoke up and broke the moment, "Stop being a prat Mark, come on Zara," and she took Zara's arm, pushed Mark's legs to one side with her own, and led Zara out from the table.

They left the pub and started to walk down the street in the direction of Zara's flat.

"What did you ever see in that man? He's like a big child and will likely never grow to be a man," Jo said as they walked arm in arm together.

"It seemed good at the time, but I was a kid then. First love and first sexual experience, I guess I just got caught up in it all. It seemed like a story out of one of the teen magazines and I just went along with it," Zara said remembering the quick hot kisses and gropes behind the girls toilets at the youth club.

"I much prefer the adult Zara," Jo said giving Zara's arm a squeeze "You stood up to him and I never remember you doing that when you were a kid. Mind you, I had to jump in as I thought I saw your knees buckle when he gave you that kicked puppy expression."

"They did not buckle," Zara said in a defensive tone. "I just felt a little sorry for him. Nobody likes rejection. If you remember rightly, he was the pretty boy of the school year and wasn't used to girls saying no, it was probably a first for him."

"You wouldn't reject me, would you, Zara," Jo purred into Zara's ear.

"Never," Zara replied. "Anyway I have a surprise for you back at my place. I've been trying to tell you all evening. Come on." They headed off down the street to Zara's flat and her surprise.

Inside the apartment Zara had poured them both a glass of red wine, "Not as powerful as the Artist's wine but just as delicious. Cheers," Zara clinked her glass with Jo.

Jo was sitting on Zara's settee looking at the photograph. Zara sat down next to her and said, "Quite a painting, eh? I would go as far as to say we look pretty good together, my lovely."

She smiled, sipped her drink and turned to face Zara. "Are you sure we only slept? I seem to remember something else?"

"I have a vague memory too. We were just so relaxed and exhausted after the day in the shops. Maybe we needed to lay together and be as one. A sort of female bonding. I think Didiet could sense this and that is why he kept saying 'be natural'; it's a memory that will stay in my mind forever," Zara replied.

"And mine," Jo said simply looking back at Zara.

Zara leant forward and placed her lips full onto Jo's, feeling their soft fullness yield to her kiss. Her tongue eased into Jo's mouth where she teased her tongue's tip with her own.

Jo let the photograph drop to the floor and raised her arm to Zara's face, stroking her cheek with her fingertips.

Zara moved away and took Jo's glass of wine from her, and placed it onto the table, "I would like to replace those missed hours now Jo, if you are in agreement?"

Jo nodded, saying nothing. Nothing needed to be said. Zara stood up unzipped her dress and removed it, leaving her only in her panties.

Zara took Jo's hand and kissed her fingers, her palm and then her wrist, where she let her tongue slide over Jo's skin and up to the inside of her elbow, that most precious erogenous zone that was so easily forgotten. Jo shivered in anticipation as Zara's tongue travelled up her arm to reach her neck. Zara slid Jo's top up and over her head leaving her white breasts half displayed over the top of her bra; she pulled the shoulder straps of the bra down over Jo's shoulders, enabling Zara to then release Jo's beautiful pale breasts tipped with her delicious rosebud nipples.

Zara kissed both of the buds, sucking each gently into her lips where she could feel them harden, and she teased them with her tongue's tip. Jo's breathing increased and she tipped her head back, arching her back in encouragement.

Zara felt for the hem of Jo's skirt and rolled it upwards to expose her pale yellow panties; she hooked her fingers under, and felt the rough curls of Jo's pubic hair. Zara traced her fingers down the, neatly trimmed, triangle of curls until she reached the bare, silken skin of Jo's moist lips; she slid the tip of her index finger into the moisture to dampen it and moved the finger to Jo's clitoris, where she proceeded to gently encircle the hard nub, around and around.

Zara looked up into Jo's face and asked, "You like?"

Jo groaned, "Mmmmm, I like."

Zara returned her mouth to Jo's breasts, licking and sucking each nipple in turn. She heard Jo's groans deepen as her finger increased its pace. Zara moved over Jo's body so that her breasts were lying over Jo's, their nipples touching. Her finger rubbed harder with the increasing speed and she could see that Jo was nearing climax so she again lowered her mouth to kiss her passionately. At that moment Jo climaxed and Zara felt the ripple of orgasm with her tongue deep inside Jo's mouth, tasting every wave.

Zara lay over Jo, her head now resting against Jo's. She could feel Jo's heartbeat against her own and Jo's hand stroking her back in slow rhythmic movements.

"Wow Zara, I think you certainly replaced those missing moments. Thank you," Jo said. "We must do this again sometime."

CHAPTER TWELVE

Five weeks had gone by since the trip to Paris and apart from that wonderful Saturday night spent with Jo, Zara had not fulfilled her sexual needs. She enjoyed Jo's body but deep down she knew it was a man that she most desired. Sex with Jo was beautiful but it did not give her the roughness that she craved. 'I need a man that can be romantic, but can also dominate me at the drop of a hat,' Zara was thinking to herself, during her lunch break. 'Is it too much to ask to find a gentleman that has the wit and intelligence to know when a girl needs to be dominated and desired? For him to take control during sex and reveal the sensual fiery depths that I know are deep inside me. Am I asking the impossible? Surely there is a man out there with all these assets? I will not take second best. I know what I want and I am going to look for it,' Zara decided but felt a little half-hearted in her chances of finding it. The telephone rang and made her jump back into the real world.

"Hello. Zara Hardcastle speaking. How may I help you?"

"Zara, Hello. It's Philippe here. We met and had lunch in Paris. Noel Dickens introduced us, remember?"

Zara remembered alright. That was her last encounter with Noel, who she still thought about. "Philippe, yes of course I remember you. How are you?"

"All the better for hearing your voice. I hope you can rescue me. I have a small dilemma; my personal assistant has gone off sick and I have important shows to attend in a few days time. Have you a professional person, who can take notes, type them up and circulate them to the right people, whilst also having computer knowledge not to mention having the ability to put up with designers' tantrums and my company? Please say you have someone available at such short notice. Oh, and obviously they must be able to speak French..."

"Hang on Philippe," Zara interrupted "Stop and take a deep breath. You are speaking so fast, I cannot keep up with you. I am sure I can help you. Run through your needs again, but slowly this time."

"Oh, Zara. You are an angel. I need a French speaking Personal assistant. A diplomat that can work under pressure," Philippe's voice took on a calmer note as he explained the duties that the job would involve. "It will only be for three or four days. I cannot manage on my own as I have some very important people to impress. You can see what a dilemma I have. I am so glad you gave me your business card and besides it was a good excuse to hear your voice again."

"Flattery will get you nowhere, it's the bank drafts that do that," Zara quipped back in response to Philippe's comment.

"I will sort a bank transfer immediately. Tell me your price and I will give my bank instructions to make a deposit into your company's account today."

"Slow down Philippe. You are no longer desperate; I can sort your problem. We had an extremely efficient person start with our company last month, Martin is his name. I am sure he will handle everything perfectly for you..."

Philippe broke into Zara's sentence, "He! I cannot possibly work with a 'he'. It must be a woman."

Philippe sounded shocked. Zara thought how old fashioned he was! She knew Martin could cope with this, after all, he had put up with T and M Merchandise and their old fashioned ways. "Well he's the only person available at such short notice, I'm afraid."

"A man it will have to be then," Philippe accepted the offer grudgingly. "But in the mean time if a beautiful lady should brighten your staff, think of me Zara."

Zara laughed, "I'll carry out some enquiries to see if I can move anyone around and then get back to you; first you must give me all the details of when you need somebody and the entire minutia so that I can quote you a fee."

They sorted out all of the information that they needed, exchanged a few pleasantries and said their goodbyes.

Zara replaced the phone, took a deep breath and buzzed Sheila's office on the intercom, "Shelia, I have a new client for you. He's worth a few grand, are you interested?"

Sheila was in Zara's office before Zara had taken her finger off the buzzer.

"Who?" Sheila demanded on entry.

"A gentleman I met in Paris, he needs someone the day after tomorrow to fly over and help him for four days maximum. I thought of your new guy, Martin, who has just finished with T and M; he's available at present."

"Fantastic idea. I told you he would be an asset to the company, didn't I? Have you checked he holds the client's requirements?"

"Here are the requirements," she handed them over for Shelia to peruse and searched to find Martin's details on her pc.

Shelia scanned Philippe's requests, "French language. I don't remember that on his CV, I think

Martin only speaks German, Urdu and Mandarin, which was one of the things I found exceptional and why I called him in for interview, by the way."

Zara had located Martin's personal details and frowned, "You're right, no French language stated here. We can't send Martin." Zara pulled up all their temps with French language skills onto her screen and cast her eye through them. This could be a money maker. She didn't want to lose this contract, and besides it could broaden their arena into International status. What could she do? Zara's thoughts were flying through her mind.

Shelia passed the requirements file back to Zara and said, "If what you say about this contract is true, we cannot afford to lose it. We also need to send an experienced professional person there, which is obviously you especially since you know the gentleman concerned." Shelia turned her back and headed for the door.

"Shelia wait. I hardly know the man. I was only in his presence for a couple of hours; you can hardly define that as knowing someone, can you?"

"You obviously impressed him in those two hours, for him to call you like this. Anyway, he's probably sorted the transfer for the fee by now." Shelia's hand was on the door to Zara's office when she turned her head and said over her shoulder, "You did take the contract without checking who could meet the requirements and therefore I feel it is up to you to cover your error."

"Point taken; I'll sort it but can you spare me?" Zara said feeling very guilty.

"When there's money to be made, I can spare anyone. If my mother could speak French, I'd send her."

"You really are a mercenary."

"In this business you have to be. Right, call him back, get the payment sorted, get that hotel and flight booked and get your suitcase packed." Shelia left the room and closed the door behind her.

Zara sat staring at the door. 'What have I let myself in for?' she thought. It had been two years since she had been a personal assistant but she had no qualms about her ability to do the job; it was Philippe that she was concerned about. It had been obvious that he was interested in her but she had not taken him seriously as she had been too busy teasing Noel. Did she fancy him? He was good looking granted but she had no physical attraction towards him. She gave herself a mental shake. 'Stop worrying,' she told herself. 'You are going to be in his employ, business and pleasure do not mix, and any good business person knows that.' And with the last disciplined thought, she sorted the papers on her desk and proceeded to call Philippe to confirm the arrangements.

The flight over was short with no complications. In Paris she was met by a chauffeur driven car and taken to her hotel. The chauffeur, whose name was Bernardot, told her that he was Philippe's driver and would be available for her use whenever he was not required by Philippe. He was a very friendly French man whom Zara discovered was a granddad of fourteen, and very proud of this fact too. She chatted quite comfortably with him in French to give her some practice and learnt a little more about Philippe's busy work schedule. Bernardot held much respect for Philippe and Zara gathered from their chit chat that Philippe was a good man to work for.

Bernardot dropped her off at her hotel where she was met by a porter that took her bags and led her to reception. Zara booked herself in and was escorted to her room by the porter. This was all so different to the hotel that she and Jo had stayed in. Philippe's company certainly looked after their staff. 'I could get used to this treatment,' she thought. Philippe had given her the hotel details with the room already booked.

The porter put her bags down, asked her to call room service if she was in need of anything, gave her the key- card and politely left.

Zara looked around her at the resplendent furnishings. The decor was in the style of Louis XV, made up of green and gold with the furniture being the same, curvy with cream and gold ornamentation. There were great swags of heavy green and gold material covering the windows and the carpet was so lush that Zara had the urge to remove her shoes and let her toes feel its depth. With her thought on just that, Zara walked over to a chair by the small desk where she could remove her shoes and stockings. On the desk was an envelope addressed to her. She opened it and read...

Zara,

So pleased your man cannot speak French.

Hope you like the free sample.

Yours, Philippe.

Free sample? Zara looked around. On the beautiful canopied bed was a box. Zara lifted the lid. Inside was pink tissue paper. Zara unfolded the paper and found within it some deep pink satin material. Zara let the material slip through her fingers, then she picked it up and held it out in front of her. A card fell onto the bed, landing written side up, it said, 'Sweet Dreams!'

Zara looked back at the nightdress; it was beautiful and felt so slinky. She smiled as she thought, 'So glad you couldn't speak French, Martin. Pink probably wouldn't have suited you anyway.'

"Work," she said out loud as she walked back to the table where she had placed the portfolio Bernardot had given her. Inside was a detailed account of what was expected of her, including a dress code. It seemed appearance was as important as the job to be done. She turned the pages and discovered a very heavy work load; it was not going to be as much fun as she had hoped. The last page held her interest though, a party to celebrate the opening of this season's lingerie. All were expected to attend and escorts would be provided for any ladies without their own.

Zara reminded herself of the time and made moves to unpack her luggage and ready herself for her work.

Promptly at 3pm, the car appeared. Bernardot drove her to a large tower block. The portfolio had said Philippe's office was on the sixteenth floor, so she headed for the lift. She stood watching the lights move across the numbers: sixteen, this was her stop. She smoothed her pale grey suit skirt, and walked out of the lift and into Philippe's arms.

"Zara, I cannot tell you how grateful I am," Philippe said holding her shoulders and kissing her on both cheeks. He straightened his arms and held her out in front of him, casting his eyes over her. "You look wonderful. Have you ever thought about modelling?"

Zara's mind quickly flashed back to the artist's studio, but she said, "Not my calling, Philippe."

They walked into Philippe's office where he explained the outline of the meeting they were attending in an hour's time.

CHAPTER THIRTEEN

Zara was exhausted by the end of her second day working as Philippe's personal assistant. The first day had been quite easy as it had just involved her paying attention and taking notes ready to type up. The second was more involved; she had to meet several of Philippe's clients at certain shows and take their orders for the new season's lingerie, attend conferences and be pleasant to everyone which included the models. Zara now held a great respect for models; she had seen the pressure they had to work under. They had to change clothes within seconds at times and were pushed and pulled about as though they were mannequins, meanwhile having to look beautiful at all times.

Her day had started at 7.30am, it was now 7pm and she had only just finished sorting out tomorrow's appointments. Bernardot had put up with her mutterings in the car where she had been trying to collate some notes on the way back from a show. Now back at the office, she was just uploading the last of those notes into their relevant files on the company's system. She gave her desk a quick tidy all the while dreaming of the welcoming hot soak in the luxury bathroom of the hotel, picked up some papers for Philippe to peruse and knocked gently on his door before entering quietly.

Philippe was on the telephone and signalled for her to take a drink whilst she was waiting. Zara placed some ice in two glasses and proceeded to pour them both a small, but well needed, shot of whisky.

"No, I don't know who yet. Huxley will probably have someone in mind for me," Philippe was saying to the person on the line. "Corinne? You lucky bastard. How did you manage to get her?"

Zara took the two glasses over to Philippe's desk, passed one to Philippe and sat in the opposite chair.

"Don't you? Well you are the only man in Paris who doesn't, I certainly would. Tell you what, we can swap half way through the evening..." Philippe's laughter reverberated around the room. "I'll see you there then, and don't forget me and mine if you need a change. Bye," Philippe replaced the receiver and took a mouthful of his drink. "Just what I needed; you are an angel, Zara. Have you finished?"

"Yes. There're just these few letters for you to check and sign," Zara said passing the papers over to Philippe to read.

"They can wait until the morning. I think we've earned a well deserved meal at your hotel," Philippe stood up, putting his jacket on. "Come on we haven't had a chance to talk socially yet."

Zara put the empty glasses back on the small bar and followed him out, "That sounds like a wonderful idea, but I really need a bath and to change first."

"No problem. I'll get Bernardot to drop you first and then I'll meet you in the hotel bar around 9.30pm. Does that suit you?"

"Fine by me. Thank you."

They both left the office and headed for the waiting car.

Zara had a long luxurious soak and felt totally refreshed. She had looked at herself in the full length mirror; the dress she had chosen to wear was of an oriental style, blue painted silk, with a high neck; her hair was piled up on her head in a Japanese comb and the high blue silk stilettos completed her look. She had asked herself why she was dressing up, and answered herself, 'Because I can,' and laughed at her own flippant reply.

Philippe was chatting to the barman when Zara arrived.

"Wow! That's a bit different to the floral number you wore on our last meal together. I'm not joking when I say you ought to think about modelling as a career, you are really beautiful Zara," Philippe said appraisingly.

Zara felt herself blush. She had forgotten about the summer frock that she had been wearing on that last day of the holiday. Philippe had not seen her socially since and therefore had only seen her in her work clothes, dark boring suits.

"Thank you for the compliment Philippe," Zara said as she took his arm, "but do you really think I would consider modelling as a career after all that I've seen today? I don't think so. Those women are under such pressure and besides, I most definitely could not live on rice cakes; I like my food too much"

They walked into the restaurant and were shown to a two-seater table tucked away in a cosy corner. Philippe pointed out his recommendations on the menu and Zara discovered they had the same tastes in food. They both ordered their meal with eager anticipation of the repast to come.

Zara felt very relaxed in his company and they were soon talking like old friends.

"Where were you born, Philippe? I wonder as you speak English so well and hardly have an accent."

"I was born in Somerset my name is really Phillip but Philippe has a better ring to it, don't you think?" Philippe asked giving an artistic wave with his hand.

Zara laughed, "You're a con. You're not really French then, just an old English yokel," Zara said teasing him..

Philippe looked a little hurt by Zara's comment, "I am not a con, as you put it. I've been living in France for twelve years now. I've never pretended to be French, some people, like you, just presume I am and who am I to put them right?"

"It's no matter to me; you are a good business man no matter what your nationality," Zara soothed in reply.

"I hope you see me as something other than a business man, Zara," Philippe said placing his hand onto hers.

The waiter arrived with their meal and relieved Zara of having to make further comment.

Zara was starving and was tucking into her food when she noticed Philippe watching her.

"It is so good to see a woman who enjoys her food. Usually I have to put up with models playing with their food, moving it around their plates like children playing with a train track."

Zara laughed again, "As I said earlier this is why I couldn't be a model; I like my food too much."

Philippe laughed and continued eating his meal.

The rest of the meal passed with the two of them talking about their favourite foods. By the time coffee arrived, Zara and Philippe had found several common grounds.

"It is so good to share the English sense of humour again. I have thoroughly enjoyed this evening with you," Philippe said smiling at Zara.

"I have too. Thank you Phillip," Zara replied, putting the emphasis on his English name. "I bet you miss your home town and family; do you manage to get over to England very often?"

"About three times a year. I was over there last month actually and came back the same time as you visited France on your holiday. I have to join Noel in England sometimes, so I manage to see my family when over on business – perks of the job, I suppose. Would you like a night cap or has the coffee satiated you?" Philippe asked.

"No thank you, Philippe. I have to work tomorrow and my boss would not approve if I was not working to full capacity."

"I know he would not mind but if that is your choice, so be it," Philippe stood, pulling back Zara's chair to help her out.

They walked back to the foyer and waited for the lift to arrive. Philippe took her arm and walked with her into the lift.

"I will escort you to your room."

They stood patiently waiting for the lift to reach Zara's floor. The silence in the lift made Zara feel uncomfortable; she was not sure of the way she wanted the evening to end. She looked into her bag for her key card, giving herself something to occupy her. After less than a minute, which felt like an eternity, the lift opened on her floor.

At Zara's door Philippe took her in his arms to kiss her goodnight. Zara expected a kiss on both cheeks but instead received a passionate kiss on the lips. She returned the kiss.

His hands moved to her breasts and started to caress them, "You are so beautiful, Zara; I would like to see you naked," Philippe's voice full of lust spoke into her ear.

Zara's body was reacting to his touch, she felt her nipples harden but she did not want this man; she did not want to confuse the employer / employee relationship and jeopardise any future contracts. But she knew she had to be strong so she gently removed Philippe's hands telling him, "I have to work with you for two more days. I do not want to compromise our working relationship. Good night, Philippe," she found her key and opened her door.

Philippe stood looking at her. She could see the lust in his eyes along with the bulge in his trousers, but she knew business and pleasure did not mix.

Maybe when their work had finished she would feel differently, Zara thought slightly regretful.

"Goodnight Zara. I will see you tomorrow then," Philippe said looking slightly abashed but smiling in acceptance.

"Goodnight Philippe and thank you for a lovely evening," Zara went into her room closing the door behind her.

Inside she looked around her; she saw the empty bed and thought of spending the night ahead, alone. She walked to the bed and pulled back the counterpane, there was the satin nightdress. Who was going to see her in it now? She walked back to the door and opened it; she would throw caution to the wind and share the night with Philippe after all. She looked out down the corridor, no Philippe. She saw the lights above the lift going down. She was too late, he was gone, and so, it seemed, was the new 'chilled out' Zara; the old workaholic had returned.

Zara shut the door and leaning against it, she felt the warm tears run down her cheeks. Why was she crying? She didn't know, really, although deep down she felt utterly alone. It had been a stupid idea to come to Paris again, so soon after... *after what?* Nothing had happened between her and Noel. It had all been a big fantasy conjured by her loneliness. He hadn't even seemed interested in her the last time they had met. Was she feeling like this out of frustration? She was physically attracting men, as Philippe had just made obvious; why hadn't the man she most wanted to fuck made any advances? *What was it with that man?*

She started to undress; she had dressed for Philippe, she knew he was attracted to her, so why hadn't she allowed him into her room? She didn't want to mix business with pleasure. Sensible Zara had made the decision; holiday Zara may have considered the possibility of sex – but she wasn't on holiday at present. She picked up the nightdress and threw it across the room; she couldn't wear it now.

She got into bed and lay there thinking. Thoughts of Noel, held captive by the black woman – he had been Zara's for the taking, yet she had not taken him, but why? She had no answers. Tomorrow and the next day she would work hard and then she would be back in England where she could forget Noel and this lustful hold he had over her.

Zara awoke after a restless sleep. She felt awful as she dragged herself up from the pillows. It was so dark; she looked at the clock by her bed, 6.15 a.m. She got out of bed, put on her bathrobe and walked to the window where she opened the curtains to let the morning sunshine through.

Outside people were already going about their daily business; she watched the hotel's papers being delivered by a young man on a scooter. She watched as a limousine pulled up in front of the hotel and the porter open the door for two elegantly dressed ladies as they took their seats in the car and she watched as it drove away. 'Paris mornings are the same as in any other city, Zara thought. People still have to earn a living.'

She picked up the hotel phone and rang reception to ask for her continental breakfast to be brought up to her room and then she went to have a shower.

The shower helped to waken her and the breakfast had been brought in by room service whilst she was showering. Sitting down at the table she glanced through the portfolio for today's work events. A full day again. 'Good,' she thought. 'That will keep my mind off irrelevant things.' On the breakfast tray was an envelope addressed to her in Philippe's handwriting; she opened it:

Beautiful Zara,

Please forgive me. I was wrong and you were right. As the saying goes 'business is business', I hope there are no hard feelings. Maybe one day in other circumstances?

Yours, Philippe

Zara smiled, he *was* a gentleman. A full blooded male absolutely, but a gentleman also. She put the letter back in the envelope and sipped her coffee. Things did not look so bad after all.

Bernardot picked her up as usual and wished her a good morning. He said that Philippe would be at a meeting with Monsieur Huxley this morning but hoped to be back in the office during the afternoon.

Zara remembered hearing that name, during the telephone call that Philippe had been taking when she entered his office last night.

The car pulled up at the office building, she asked Bernardot who Mr Huxley was; It turned out that he was the gentleman that organised the shows and the after show parties. She thanked Bernardot, said goodbye and left the car.

Zara's desk was yet again stacked full of client's orders and enquiries, telephone messages and memos. She started to wade through the pile, paying first attention to Philippe's memos. Most were reminders of certain client's demands, Philippe liked to treat each as an individual so that all their personal needs were catered for. One memo suggested she go to the first show without him, as he did not think he would make it back in time to accompany her. He also added he was sure she knew how it all worked by now. This did not worry Zara as she knew Bernardot would transport her to the right place, Philippe had also said that each show's agenda was much the same.

Zara checked the time that she had to meet the client at today's show and put the client's file to one side ready for later. She then proceeded to work through the remaining items on her desk making notes for Philippe's perusal this afternoon.

The show was only a small one, compared to the few that Zara had already attended. The models were wearing the new season's colour, 'blush', as the company had called it, a soft reddish pink colour.

Zara stood just inside the door of the auditorium watching the girls readying their selves for the gangway parade of beautiful lingerie as she waited for her client. One blonde model was wearing the nightdress that Philippe had given Zara; her stomach did a flip as she thought of the night before.

"That would look much better on a brunette, don't you think?" A voice said quietly in her ear.

She felt the warm breath and smelt the aroma of 'Aramis' therefore before she looked, she knew it was him, her infatuation and desire, and this time she would not let him slip away. She turned and smiled warmly, looking directly into his eyes she said, "This season's colour 'blush', though beautiful on most women I am sure, would probably bring out the worst in someone with my skin tone,' she said in the best advertising voice she could muster. "Hello Noel."

Noel took her hand and kissed her gently on both cheeks saying good humouredly, "I would like to see the worst of you sometime," and he led her towards the two reserved seats at the back of the auditorium and invited her to sit.

"I am waiting for my client, you will have to leave when they arrive, Zara said looking anxiously towards the door.

I *am* your client or rather my company is. I'm sorry I'm a little late but I got caught in traffic." Noel sat beside Zara. "So you're the temp that Philippe acquired at such short notice? He certainly kept that quiet."

Zara opened her client's file and took out the order forms, "Your name is not mentioned here; are you supposed to be here?," Zara felt that she ought to be doing her job in a proper manner and did not want to make any mistakes.

"The gentleman that you were expecting has had to attend another meeting and he asked me to step in for him. I am extremely happy that I could oblige, otherwise I would not have known you were here. I am over here for this season's lingerie shows - we were obviously destined to meet again, don't you agree Zara?" Noel ran his fingertips over her hand holding the file.

Zara's skin tingled where she felt his touch, "Destiny cannot be avoided," she replied whilst thinking, 'I mustn't mess this chance up.'

Together they watched the show with Zara jotting down the garments that Noel commented on or showed interest in, taking the orders he placed also.

After the show, Noel led Zara to the refreshment table and they discussed the orders he had made.

"'I would like to see one particular garment again. Number 36, I think it was; could you find it for me again please?" Noel asked her.

"I have never been asked to do that before. How do I go about it?" Zara felt a little useless and was glad it was Noel asking and not someone she did not know.

"Usually you find the model that wore it and ask her to repeat but I am sure the models are exhausted now, and besides I would much prefer you to model it for me. Would you, Zara?"

Zara felt flustered and lost her cool business manner, thinking this was another opportunity on offer that she must not let pass. She looked at Noel, his blue eyes piercing right through her and she felt her knees go weak with the lust she felt for him. "Where do I go to find number 36?" Zara heard her voice betray her need for him and judging by the look in his eyes, the feeling was mutual.

"I take it that's a yes." Noel said with a great emphasis on the 'yes', "This way," Noel led Zara around to the back of the gangway to the model's changing area.

The models had all dispersed for a break before the next show but the garments were all hanging on the rails, labelled and bagged. Noel found number 36 and handed it to Zara. The place was now silent, completely empty of people who had better things to do than hang around in their place of work.

"Where do I change?" Zara asked, looking around for a screen for some privacy.

"Where all the models do. Here," Noel's reply was quite curt; almost an order and Zara felt a thrill of danger ripple through her veins. She could feel the attraction manifesting between them and knew this was the beginning of what she had been craving from him all along.

"In front of you?'" she asked. "Someone might come in."

"The models have to dress and redress in front of me all of the time; we are all used to it." Noel leant back against the wall with his arms folded watching Zara intently.

Zara placed the file on the floor and started to unzip her skirt. She could feel Noel's eyes scrutinising her every movement; she could see that he was enjoying this. This was the sexual dominance that she had been craving; she trusted him ultimately as he had proven to her with his actions that he was a gentleman, but she also felt fear, or was it actually excitement that she felt? From the thrill of him taking control? Either way this was turning her on immensely and she wasn't going to miss yet another chance to fuck this man.

Her skirt fell around her ankles as she slowly unbuttoned her blouse; she stood in her underwear as she unzipped the bag that held garment number 36. Pulling it out, she saw that it was a half cupped bodice with the shade of 'blush' covering the cups, leaving the remainder of the garment white. Zara started to put her feet into the leg holes, when Noel interrupted her.

"It is underwear. You will have to remove the underclothes you are wearing first, for me to appreciate it fully on your body," Noel said in his dictatorial manner. He moved in front of Zara and reached behind her to undo her bra.

"I have had dreams of touching your naked body, Zara," Noel whispered as he unhooked the bra and slid it gently towards him, brushing his hands over the curves of her breasts as he did so.

Zara's breathing quickened, 'This man is the one for me,' she thought. 'I want him to take me here and now, hard and fast.'

After having her bra removed, Zara stood still as Noel proceeded to hook his fingers into the waistband of her panties, slide them down her long legs whilst moving downwards with them for her to step out of them. He stood up, in front of her again and leant forward to take her naked body in his arms kissing her head, face and neck.

She could feel the roughness of his suit against her smooth skin. She breathed in deeply the spicy scent of Aramis on his skin, whilst tasting the lust of his kisses.

"Put this on for me Zara," Noel's voice asked, whispering into her ear. He handed the bodice to her and Zara pulled it on. Her breasts were nearly overflowing the half cups and she stood, posing, enjoying the reaction she was seeing in Noel's eyes and body. She could see that he was feeling the same way. Their eyes held each other's and betrayed all of the unspoken words that their bodies were feeling: utter lust.

"There you are; what's this then? A private show or can anyone watch?" Philippe's voice shattered the moment in one second that had taken weeks to reach.

CHAPTER FOURTEEN

Zara turned and saw Philippe staring greedily at her mostly naked body, and looked around for a wrap or something to cover herself with.

Noel's voice cut in calmly, "Zara is modelling number 36 for me, as all the models had left, so I could see it more clearly," this directed at Philippe, but to Zara he said, "Thank you Zara. I will have that garment also, mark it down on my order please." Noel walked towards Philippe and guided him back to the auditorium, "Let's leave Zara to change in peace. I want to ask you about the party tonight."

They walked away leaving Zara to dress and find some time to regain her business-like manner.

Why did Philippe have to ruin it? If only he had not arrived! Yet another opportunity missed, but at least this time it was not of her doing. There was one good thing that had come out of this though, Zara thought, she knew now that Noel wanted her as much as she wanted him. She was also aware of Philippe's attraction to her, and that put her in a difficult situation because Shelia was so desperate for Zara to make a good impression and she did not want anything to ruin future business contracts.

After Zara had dressed and regained her composure, she joined the two men in the auditorium, catching their conversation as she neared them.

"The swap is still on then. I don't know yours yet, maybe I won't like her and will prefer to stay with Corinne for the whole evening," Noel was saying in a teasing tone of voice.

"Yeah, but I'm not so sure I want Corinne anymore. *My* date may be more to my choosing," Philippe replied.

Zara joined the men, now feeling more level headed yet quite frustrated. If she didn't get fucked soon, she thought she might just die.

"Would you like a drink Zara, before we head back to the office?" Philippe asked as he passed Noel a coffee taken from the percolator on the refreshment table.

She didn't want to go back to the office yet. She wanted to talk to Noel in private to find out more. She didn't know how long he was in the country for or when he was returning to England and most importantly they hadn't exchanged mobile phone numbers. If she wasn't able to fuck him in France, she hoped she'd at least be able to meet up with him in good ole Blighty for a romp. All this and more was going through her mind when she replied, "Thank you. I'll just have a small coffee to keep me going until we return."

Philippe worked the machine and passed her a small creamy latte. "We only have to collate today's orders and then we can ready ourselves for the new season's party tonight. Have you something to wear this evening, Zara, or would you like to borrow something from our main store?"

Zara could feel Philippe's eyes burning through her clothes: she could see that he was undressing her in his mind and this made her feel uncomfortable in front of Noel. "I brought a dress with me, thank you Philippe. I got it in Paris though, when I was here on holiday actually, so it should be most suitable," Zara replied quite coolly, hoping to distract those eyes from her body. She turned to Noel and asked, "Are you attending the party too, or will you be 'tied up' again?"

Noel's eyes sparkled with amusement as he clicked straight away as to what Zara was eluding to. "I shall be attending and I will look forward to seeing you there."

"You may be otherwise distracted tonight Noel," Philippe cut in, then said with a wink in Noel's direction, "Corinne."

Zara's mind was triggered back to a phone conversation yesterday and connected Philippe's newest comment to it and the end of the overheard conversation today. 'They're talking about the date swap I bet. Men, they're all the same. I pity the poor women involved,' she thought.

Philippe and Zara finished their drinks and headed back to the office.

After Zara uploaded her notes and the orders onto the computer, she readied the next day's work for Philippe's Personal Assistant since she was returning having now recovered. Zara checked that everything was in order and that she had not disturbed any of the items in her work place and was pleased to see that she was ready to leave.

"I shall miss your efficient work Zara. I am very pleased with the way you have taken everything on board whilst you have been here. I shall write to your manager and thank her for being willing to muddle through without you in the office," Philippe told Zara as they left the office and were walking to the car.

"I have enjoyed the change and am glad that you are pleased with my work. I do hope you will use our services again in the future Philippe."

"No doubt about that," Philippe said as he opened the car door for Zara. "I haven't told you yet, who your escort for tonight's party is, have I?"

"I was unaware that I was in need of an escort, but as this is your party and obviously your rules, I hope it isn't anyone too boring," Zara said when they were both sitting in the car. She was mindful of some of the designers she had met during the last week and knew that watching paint dry would be more exciting then spending a night with them.

Philippe's phone rang and he muttered his excuses and took the call. Zara looked out of the car window watching as the familiar buildings passed, thinking that she was unlikely to see them again any time soon at least.

The car pulled up at Zara's hotel and as she got out, Philippe interrupted his call to speak to her, "You will be collected from your hotel at 8pm; don't eat too much as the dinner provided is usually excellent. Your escort will definitely not be boring; these parties are rarely boring anyway, but I know your escort very well and he is one of the best. I'll see you at eight then. Bye for now," Philippe said as he closed the door behind her.

Zara watched as the car drove away. Philippe was to be her escort then. Her mind recollected the two men's conversation again. No way was she going to be part of their little 'swap' plans. She was not a toy that could be played with. The cheek of men. The cheek of Noel. How dare he think that she would be a pawn in their little game? Feeling cross, she walked to the lift and then to her hotel room with her hands clenched in fists by her sides.

In her room she started to undress for a shower, thinking of the evening ahead. She thought she would not go; that would thwart their plans. She did not have to stay for the evening, her work was done here. She pulled her suitcase open and started throwing her clothes inside. She would not be used like a Barbie doll; taken out to play and passed around to someone else when a new doll was available. How dare they even think about it! The more Zara thought about it, the angrier she became.

She walked into the bathroom to turn the shower on and turned it to the cold setting. Stepping in under the freezing needles, she calmed down slightly. What would Jo do in this situation? 'She'd just deal with it,' Zara thought. As Zara washed, an idea came to her. 'I'll call Jo. I'll tell her everything; she'll know what to do.'

Zara called Jo on the hotel phone and related the situation to her, whilst also admitting to the encounter on the ferry dance floor.

"You dark horse you. All the time we were on holiday you were having sexual tit-bits and you never told me. There I was feeling sorry for you. And now you're in a pickle and want my help? Don't see why I should; serves you right," Jo was saying to Zara down the phone-line.

"Aw Jo," Zara pleaded "You know how much I respect your advice concerning men."

"Huh," Jo contended "As I recall you completely ignored me when I warned you about Mark many years ago."

"That was then. I was young and inexperienced..."

"...You're far from that now," Jo cut in. "Your trouble is, you now have the sexual experience but you don't know how to utilise it to your advantage."

Zara laughed "You cheeky madam; I seem to remember acquiring a dress from a boutique in Paris where I 'utilised my sexuality to my advantage'."

They laughed together then Jo said finally relenting her teasing, "I don't know if I agree with you about Noel being your secret dance partner, though. He doesn't seem the type to me. Besides, if it was him, wouldn't he be doing his utmost to complete what he'd started?"

Zara was listening intently, hoping desperately that Jo could help her.

"Why don't you give them some of their own treatment," Jo continued. "Why not make a play for this Corinne woman that would halt their plans?"

"I can't do that, I don't even know her, and anyway I'm not that way inclined."

"You could have fooled me. That's not the Zara that I've been recently acquainted with."

Zara could hear the disappointment in Jo's tone of voice, "You are an exception Jo. I love you and I enjoy your body, we're comfortable together. But not with, a stranger; that's completely different," Zara replied remembering their most intimate moments.

"Well, I can't help you then. Corinne is the only way out I can see. You will have to decide for yourself but I don't recommend coming home now. Sheila would not be best pleased, if you decided that course."

Zara knew that Jo was right. Sheila would be upset if she terminated the contract with bad feelings. "No, I won't leave early. I'll just have to play it by ear. Thanks Jo, it's been good to talk it all through."

"Good luck for tonight, honey. Don't worry; I'm sure you'll handle it, like an expert. Remember the 'new' Zara; she wouldn't run away from a challenge. See you when you get back when you can tell me all about it, this time not holding back any secret titbits."

Zara said goodbye and replaced the telephone receiver. She sat, still in her towel, on the bed thinking of her options. No way could she make a move on an unknown woman. But Jo might be onto something. She *could* make a move on a man that she knew. Philippe was definitely interested in her. If she wore her 'free' scarlet dress, the one that had helped to transform her into this new liberated female, she would be able to make him see only her and not want Corinne. And that would put a spanner in the works. That would show them that she was not just some puppet in their sexist theatre. She would use this new sexual power that had been awakened and she would play the role of puppet master, not puppet.

Zara spent a long time readying herself for her evening. She took the scarlet dress off its hanger and held it up in front of her and looked in the mirror; *'If this didn't do the trick, nothing would,'* she thought. She knew that she could not wear anything under this dress; it was designed to be worn like a second skin. Zara ran her fingers up the slit in the side, which she knew would show just enough whilst leaving just enough to the imagination. 'Just enough to tease,' she thought smirking to herself.

After she put her lipstick onto the dressing table, she stood up and viewed herself in the full length mirror. She was pleased with the result, especially her hair; she had used her curling tongs to give a soft curl to the ends and the long black strands fell softly over her shoulders, slightly covering her skin that was glowing in anticipation. She was quite aware of how low cut the dress was, plunging down deep into her cleavage. This dress was made for seduction and tonight she was ready to seduce.

There was a knock at the door and Zara looked at her watch, 8pm on the dot. 'Well here goes,' she thought, and moved slowly to open the door, making sure her facial expression showed her intent for the night to come.

CHAPTER FIFTEEN

Zara opened the door and Philippe was standing waiting.

"No more business, no more work, time to relax," Zara said with a smile as she stepped out and pulled the door closed behind her.

Philippe stood staring at Zara. He put out his arm and stopped her from walking past him. He turned her to face him and looking directly into her eyes said, "No more business, yes, after all, business and pleasure do not mix. A wise and exceedingly beautiful woman once told me. Tonight it is all about pleasure." Philippe took Zara's hands up to his lips and kissed her fingers, looking her in the eyes as he did so.

"I am not the business woman tonight. You will be escorting Zara, the woman, this evening," she said returning his gaze and remembering that she was the puppet master, not Philippe.

Philippe leant in towards Zara's face and kissed her intimately on the lips, a slow sensual kiss. Zara felt an exciting tingle in her groin and knew it was more from the devilment that she was feeling, rather than the kiss that she was receiving.

"You are so beautiful, Zara. I feel greatly privileged that I am to escort you this evening. I will be the envy of all."

They walked down the corridor and into the lift. Zara made sure that she made physical contact with Philippe at every opportunity; a brush here, a slight touch there all moved her towards her ultimate goal: thwarting their game plans.

The twenty large oval tables held twelve couples on each, with men, alternating with women, in the seating arrangements. The dining hall was vast and Zara only recognised a few faces. She was seated to the right of Philippe and on her other side was Monsieur Joudon, a designer from one of the companies she had worked with that week. Monsieur Joudon was escorting his wife who, Zara thought, looked more like his daughter. They exchanged pleasantries occasionally but most of the meal was taken up by Philippe, with his conversation and questions, who seemed utterly besotted with Zara. She was relishing in this sexual power she had discovered, along with the knowledge that she would not be a pawn in their game.

She glanced around for Noel but was unable to locate him in the sea of faces. She was eager to meet Corinne too, the woman that Philippe supposedly wanted so much. By the time the coffee arrived, Philippe had his hand placed on Zara's bare thigh that had been exposed by the slit in her dress.

"Did you enjoy the meal Zara? I see that you ate well again," Philippe said whilst stroking her thigh under the table.

Zara placed her hand on top of his, running her fingers over his, "Yes, thank you Philippe. It was excellent, as you said it would be."

Philippe un-wrapped a mint, and offered to place it into her mouth. "Have I told you how divine you look tonight?"

Zara took the offered mint, sensually sucking it from his fingers and letting her tongue trail against a fingertip. She watched his pupils dilate at her touch. 'Jo would be proud of me,' she thought. 'I have him in my web, well and truly tangled now.'

During the speeches and the couple presentations, Philippe's persistence did not let up. Zara received 'sweet nothings' in her ear along with his fingertip's touching right up to her hip and the top of the split in her dress. Finally Mr Huxley took the microphone and thanked everybody for their hard work, and inviting them to relax and enjoy the remainder of the evening.

"Shall we join the dancers in the other room? It's more private in there," Philippe said standing up and offering Zara his arm.

"Yes, let's," Zara said simply and slowly.

They left the dining table and walked together towards the large dance hall that led out to the garden beyond, via large French doors that were open to let the warm summer air inside.

They stopped near to the bar. When Philippe went to fetch them both a drink, Zara had a chance to search for Noel, but again had no joy in locating him. She walked to the large glass doors that opened out to the garden and stood watching the couples dance. There were beautiful women everywhere. Normally she would have felt out of place in amongst so many gorgeous women, but this new image along with her new dress gave her the confidence to be the person that she looked; and she knew she was radiant.

Philippe returned with the drinks and a young man and woman.

"This is Zara, who I was telling you about. Zara meet Jean and Brigitte."

Zara followed the French custom of kissing both cheeks and laughed when Jean commented on her actions as being, 'Most un-British.'

"When in Rome. Anyway I think it is a much more pleasant way of greeting than a stuffy old handshake," Zara said immediately feeling warmed by this couple's light-hearted manner.

"So you are the lady that has rescued Philippe in his hour of need," Brigitte was saying. "I bet he will miss you when you return to England." Brigitte took

Zara's arm and started to lead her away, saying over her shoulder to the men, "We are just going to powder our noses, be back in a moment."

They walked together to the powder room, Brigitte holding Zara's arm as they walked, "How long have you been helping Philippe?"

"Just these last three days. His personal assistant has been unwell and my company stepped in to assist. How do you know him?" Zara asked, interested in gaining some broader knowledge of the company and its associates for future contracts.

"I don't really. My husband Jean works with him, but in the sales department. I'm only here as I wouldn't leave Jean alone with all these beautiful models around, especially not, after a few drinks."

"Oh, I'm sure you have nothing to worry about. You are absolutely beautiful and, anyway, he works with them. It must get a little mundane after a while dealing with models day in, day out," Zara replied meaning what she said; Brigitte was a stunner.

"Yes, he frequently mentions the boredom of having to work with gorgeous women all of the time," Brigitte said ironically. "But eh, there must be worse jobs." Brigitte and Zara laughed together. "Anyway, what do you think of Philippe? I hope he is behaving himself."

Zara told her that she was only in town on business and until tonight they had not spent much time together socially. The women reached the powder room, which was a large comfortably furnished room that Zara thought was nicer and larger than the 'best' room in her parents' house. It had floor to ceiling mirrors with a shelved wall unit, which contained powder puffs, tissues, wipes and creams aplenty. There were several ladies there, too, touching up their make-up.

"See that lady over there," Brigitte nodded in the direction of a beautiful platinum blonde in a short silver dress. "That's the famous, Corinne," she said in a hushed voice. "I expect you've heard her name mentioned a few times. She is Paris' top model at the moment, in fact, Jean tells me that Philippe has had his eye on her."

"Yes, I heard him talking about her on the telephone to someone the other day," Zara said seeing Corinne's legs in the mirror behind her; they seemed to go on for ever. "Do you think he'll strike it lucky tonight?"

"If he plays his cards right. I saw her arrive with Noel Dickens earlier, and I doubt if he is here for anything other than the presentations. He didn't seem the slightest bit impressed that he was her escort for the evening."

'How very interesting,' Zara thought. She had always imagined Noel living it up in this glamorous world, but the reality was sounding a lot different from the fantasy. "I met Noel today at a show; he seemed like quite a nice person." Zara watched

Brigitte apply her lipstick and asked, "Do you know him well?"

"Not very well, I only see him at these parties, and he's never done anything that has gotten him mentioned in the gossip circles."

Zara could see Corinne behind her in the mirror and could understand Philippe's attraction to her. She smiled as she thought of Jo's suggestion and could just imagine what Jo would do in the same situation.

"Well that's me done; shall we join the men again?" Brigitte asked zipping up her small clutch bag. They made for the exit together.

Jean and Philippe were in deep conversation when they returned and Zara felt relieved that they now had company. She was fast going off the role as puppet master, now that she had gained further information of Noel's personality. She had not forgotten that she was a pawn in their game though. She still felt angry about that, but the edge had been taken away from her irritation somehow.

Brigitte broke up the men's conversation by insisting on Jean accompanying her in a dance. This left Zara and Philippe alone again.

"Shall we join them Zara?" Philippe asked with a twinkle in his eye.

Zara enjoyed the music and discovered that Philippe was not a bad dancer. In fact she found herself smiling and laughing with him as they tried different moves together. During one dance Philippe was dancing behind her, holding her in his arms close to his chest. He pushed his body up against her back and started to move with her in a sensually erotic manner.

At that moment, everything clicked into place. Zara's mind returned to another dance in a different place and in another time sphere, but with the same man. This was her stranger, her intimate dance partner on the ferry. It had not been Noel, but Philippe, who had aroused her on the dance floor, she was sure of it. He must have been there with Noel on the ferry.

Philippe had started to kiss the back of her neck and was whispering into her ear. Zara dragged herself back to the present to hear what he was saying.

"The rhythm's not quite the same is it?" Philippe was whispering huskily.

Zara froze. It all made complete sense now. Philippe and Noel had used her as their 'plaything' on the ferry and they had planned to use her again tonight. Zara was fuming. How dare they.

She broke away from Philippe's hold saying harshly, "I need a drink," and she headed for the bar. As she stood stiffly waiting for Philippe to get her drink, Noel appeared.

"Hello, are you both enjoying yourselves?" he asked breezily.

Zara glared at him, took her drink from Philippe and tried to gain some composure.

"I am, but I'm not sure whether Zara is," Philippe replied nodding in Zara's direction. "Are you feeling alright Zara?" he asked with a smirk on his face.

Zara felt her anger building up inside her as she saw the smirk on Philippe's face. 'He thinks he's got me hot and ready for him. He thinks my anger is passion for him. The stupid idiot,' Zara thought bitterly but said cuttingly, "Not really Philippe. I think I need a breath of fresh air to clear my head." She turned and walked towards the open French Windows.

Noel watched as Zara headed for the doors and stopping Philippe from following her he asked, "What's happened?"

"I think she's just worked out who her dancing partner was on the ferry," Philippe said bluntly and continued. "I'll sort it out," he started to follow Zara but Noel held onto his arm.

"Sometimes you are a real bastard, Philippe. She's too good for your little games. You should have told her the truth. Besides she's not your *type*. Piss off and find Corinne, maybe she likes 'playing games'.

Leave me to deal with Zara," Noel said trying to keep his voice down.

"Got a soft spot for her have you? There I was starting to think you were celibate, for all the interest you've shown in Corinne," Philippe replied sneeringly.

"Unlike you, I don't like my women looking and acting like glorified Barbie dolls, I prefer a good conversation and a challenge," Noel said as he walked away from Philippe and headed for the garden after Zara.

Zara had found a small gazebo at the bottom of the gardens, tucked away behind a tall topiary hedge. She stood with her eyes blazing and her lips taut; she was feeling frustrated and angry. The breeze was cool on her face but was not relieving the heat of the anger she felt inside. Her thoughts were collecting all the information that she had missed, or rather that she had been unaware of at the time. She remembered Noel saying 'we' had to catch the ferry and had vaguely wondered who he was travelling with, but other things had kept her distracted. Noel was just as bad as Philippe. He had led her to believe that he was her strange dance partner; why had he done that? Zara's thoughts were interrupted by Noel's arrival.

"You're upset," Noel said arriving to stand just outside the gazebo.

"Damned right I am," Zara said angrily, "I hope you both rot in hell. Is this how you both get your kicks? Leading women on and using them as pawns in your childish games. Well count me out; I don't want to play," Zara spat at Noel, as she walked past him, heading towards the steps, leading down onto the lawn.

"Not so fast," Noel said as he grasped Zara's wrist, preventing her departure. "This afternoon we were rudely interrupted. I would like to continue where we left off."

Zara was halted in her tracks. 'How dare he,' she thought gritting her teeth in anger. She spun around to face him and threw the remaining drink from her glass into his face.

Noel's next action happened so fast that Zara could not prepare herself in defence. He snatched the glass from her hand, threw it over the railings onto the grass below; spun her around and pinned her between his body and the railings of the gazebo.

Zara looked down at the glass on the lawn, she could not struggle as Noel was holding her arms behind her back and was using his weight to keep her trapped.

"Now listen to me," he said lightening his grasp on her wrists slightly. "You have totalled up two and two and made five. Don't assume that I have anything to do with Philippe's game playing. I don't play games," his voice was deep and serious, making a shiver run through Zara's body.

"You don't have any right; let me go," Zara tried to move but Noel held her body trapped still by his own. Zara could feel herself respond to the hold he had on her; she could feel the adrenalin coursing through her veins and the heat between her thighs was not from anger. She found that she was greatly aroused by his actions. Was this the rough that she had been craving?

"I am aware I don't have any rights over you or any other woman. But answer me this, do you or don't you feel the same way I do?"

Zara turned her head to look at him; her dark eyes stared deep into his sharp blue ones and she realised that this was not part of the game. This was Noel, the man that she was destined to meet. The gentleman that had never stepped over the line. The quiet man that had been patiently waiting for her to say yes.

"I can show you how much I don't want you and you can show me how much you don't want me," Noel said huskily letting go of her wrists.

Zara was now free to retaliate but her body was still pushed up against the railings with Noel's body right behind her back. She did not want to retaliate; she just wanted to feel him inside her.

Zara took a gasp of air as she felt his cold fingers search for her breast, and he must have felt her excitement from her nipple's reaction, as he leant his mouth close to her neck and ear and whispered,

"Your body wants me. What about the rest of you?" His fingers tweaked and released her nipple roughly. Zara felt her knees start to shake; her body could not hide her want. It was responding without any conscious thought.

"What do you want Zara?" Noel asked again. He pushed his knee between her legs, parting them as his hand gathered a handful of her dress. He raised the dress up to her thighs and found what he was searching for.

Zara could feel his cold fingers slip inside her, easily; he roughly explored her hot need. She pushed her rear backwards towards his groin. She felt the cool air blow against her exposed breast, teasing her erect nipple and she melted into his hold.

"Say it Zara, I can stop or I can continue. Do you want me?" Noel asked with his warm breath soothing the skin on her neck.

"I want you Noel," Zara breathed out pleadingly.

That was all Noel needed to hear. He took a step backwards and pushed her body gently forwards so she was leaning over the railings. He raised her dress to her waist and looked at her, legs straddled, exposed and waiting for him to enter her.

"Fuck me Noel, please, now," she gasped as her own fingers found her wetness and started to work on her frustration.

Noel removed her fingers and replaced them with his hard cock. She felt him enter her, slowly, but with firmness, until he completely filled her. He waited, not moving. Zara could feel him pulsing inside of her, he was as close to orgasm as she was. She knew this would not last long as they were both so desperate for the release of this longed for union.

Noel started to thrust into her and Zara grabbed the railings to give herself some resistance to take each one of the long deep thrusts.

This was the moment that she had been waiting for for so long; the moment that she had imagined in her thoughts. Zara responded to each of Noel's movements with as much force and speed as his. She went with him willingly and raised up onto her toes, to give him all of her. She could feel both of their bodies pulsing as one and knew that they would reach their peak together. As her orgasm overtook her body Noel wrapped his arms around her and kissed her neck breathing out her name as he too felt his release.

"Why did we have to wait so long? I want to take you back to your hotel now and make love to you," Noel said after they had tidied themselves up.

"Is there a back entrance, so we can escape?" Zara replied smiling in agreement.

"There's a gate at the bottom of the lawn, we could try that way. We can slip out before anyone misses us." Noel took Zara's hand and started to lead her down over the lawn.

They left the party by the back entrance and made their way to Zara's hotel for their night of gentle exploration to discover the secret places that each of their bodies craved – a night of love-making.

CHAPTER SIXTEEN

Zara's head lay on Noel's chest. She could hear his heart beating as his chest moved slowly up and down in sleep. Her lips pressed against his blonde curls. They had spent an hour of slow love making, where Noel had shown he had a tender side. He had kissed her body all over, taking his time to touch every part of her. Her toes tingled as she remembered his tongue trailing into each crevice. There was not one part of her that he had missed. They had then slept for a while and now Zara was awake, thinking.

Would she see him again after tonight? She did not know where he lived, or for how long he was staying in Paris. She knew one thing though, she wanted to see him again. But what if she could not? She thought, 'I'll just have to make the most of his body now.'

With her body pointing downwards, her lips moved down over his chest and stomach and found what they were searching for. The tip of her tongue shot out and flicked the silken skin of his manhood and she happily received an immediate response.

As her mouth did its work, Noel's arms pulled her legs up to straddle his chest. The thumbs of both of his hands started to kneed her outer lips, and he gently lowered her legs downwards drawing her towards his face. His mouth and tongue took over from his thumbs and Zara felt herself melt to his control.

She could no longer concentrate on the pleasure she had been giving him; he was again dominating her actions. He pulled his body up, keeping her lower half in contact with his mouth. He cupped her breasts in both hands and brushed his thumbs over her nipples. Zara completely lost control of the situation and her hips moved with his tongue. She gyrated her body on his mouth, using his tongue as a pivot. Her climax overtook her unexpectedly and as it started to lessen, Noel lifted her from his face and replaced her lower down his body, impaling her on his erection.

Zara gasped as she felt him fill her. She had never made love at this angle before; she enjoyed the stimulation but was missing seeing his face.

"Don't move up and down," Noel said guiding her hips with his hands. "Just carry on rotating like you were before," Zara obeyed her instructions and slowly started to rotate her hips.

"That's beautiful Zara. It's the same movement you use when you dance; it really turns me on," Noel said softly to her.

Zara could not see his face but she could judge by his movements and breathing that this was having an effect upon him. She repeatedly, tensed and relaxed her vaginal muscles in time with her circular hip motion.

"Christ! What are you doing? It's fantastic, don't stop."

Zara continued; she liked the fact that she was now returning the pleasure that he had, only moments ago, given her. They were a perfect pair; they both had met their match and could give and receive pleasure equally.

Zara suddenly realised that she had easy access to Noel's other sensitive parts so she leant one hand down between his legs and started to rub the soft skin of his perineum. Noel's hips started to thrust upwards in excitement and just as Zara felt the knowing pulse inside her she slid one finger up into Noel's tight tunnel. She heard him cry out as his orgasm overtook his body and she smiled to herself, in the knowledge that she was able to give him that pleasure.

Noel sat up and wrapped his arms around Zara's body and stroked her hair, and kissed her neck. "I think I am falling in love with you, Zara."

Zara eased herself out of his embrace and lay down next to him. He leant in to her and kissed her intimately, "What flight are you taking home?"

Zara looked into his eyes and searched for the emotions that he had voiced – they were there, open for her to see. "The plane leaves at noon and I really have to catch it. Shelia is expecting me back. I have to leave," Zara replied not wanting to spoil the moment but knowing that she had to go.

"When can I see you again?" Noel asked her, his voice betraying his emotions.

Zara thought for a while. She was not sure that she loved Noel; she knew that she did not want to leave him, but she needed more time to think about the word 'love'. It was too soon. She wasn't sure that she wanted a steady relationship yet; not now that she had released the inner Zara – the Zara that she had not had much time to enjoy. "Should we arrange a date or just leave it to destiny again? We both seem to like life on the edge, don't we? I think it may ruin things if we start taking control and organising our futures," Zara could hardly believe she had just said it, but it was true. Her relationship with Noel worked on its unexpectedness; they had craved each other because it had taken so long to get together. She was worried that organising a date would bring routine and boredom, and that would ruin everything. Zara watched as Noel took her words in, analysed and logged them.

"You're right. What we have is special, but I don't want to lose it. Would it harm, if we nudged destiny occasionally, by making sure we were in the same city from time to time?"

"I'm sure that everybody has a hand in their own destiny at least once in a while. Why not give it a nudge? You know where I work and I know where you work; I'm sure we'll see each other again soon. Let's leave it at that and concentrate on the now. We have nine and a half hours until my flight leaves, how should we fill the time?"

Noel rolled Zara over onto her back and pinned her arms above her head, trapped her legs with his own and looked down onto her face. "Let destiny make the choice," he said pressing his mouth onto hers to stop any reply.

ABOUT THE AUTHORS

Damsel and Rogers are the writing duo of Trinity Damsel and Crystal Rogers. As friends Trinity and Crystal quickly discovered they shared two passions in life: writing and a love of the sexual. They realised the best way to enjoy those passions was to join them up to create something entirely titillating for themselves and for others.

If you enjoyed Zara's adventure, feel free to leave feedback on Amazon or email Damsel and Rogers at contact@damselandrogers.com to let them know.

Keep an eye out for further titillations; the duo is already working on the next instalment of short stories along with some more full length erotic novels.

If you enjoy DAMSEL & ROGERS, take a look at these books written by CATHERINE IONE GRAY:

SCIENCE FICTON:

The Farm

The Settlements: The Talmidge Affair

Attractions

THRILLER:

The Sight of Evil

The Colour of Evil

PLAYS:

Mono and Dia: 'Logues for a Modern World

Visit www.catherineionegray.com for more details.

Printed in Great Britain
by Amazon.co.uk, Ltd.,
Marston Gate.